Kiera Hudson & The White Wolf

(Kiera Hudson Series Three) Book 5

Tim O'Rourke

Copyright © 2015 Tim O'Rourke

All rights reserved.

ISBN: 10: 1516939085
ISBN-13: 978-1516939084

Copyright 2015 by Tim O'Rourke

This book is a work of fiction. The names, characters, places, and incidents are products of the writer's imagination or have been used fictitiously and are not to be construed as real. Any resemblance to persons, living or dead, actual events, locales or organisations is entirely coincidental.

This book is licensed for your personal enjoyment only. This book may not be re-sold or given away to other people. If you would like to share this book with another person, please purchase an additional copy for each recipient. If you're reading this book and did not purchase it, or it was not purchased for your use only, then please purchase your own copy. Thank you for respecting the hard work of this author.

Story Editor
Lynda O'Rourke
Book cover designed by:
Carles Barrios
Copyedited by:
Carolyn M. Pinard
Carolynpinardconsults@gmail.com

For Thomas O'Rourke

More books by Tim O'Rourke

Kiera Hudson Series One
Vampire Shift (Kiera Hudson Series 1) Book 1
Vampire Wake (Kiera Hudson Series 1) Book 2
Vampire Hunt (Kiera Hudson Series 1) Book 3
Vampire Breed (Kiera Hudson Series 1) Book 4
Wolf House (Kiera Hudson Series 1) Book 5
Vampire Hollows (Kiera Hudson Series 1) Book 6

Kiera Hudson Series Two
Dead Flesh (Kiera Hudson Series 2) Book 1
Dead Night (Kiera Hudson Series 2) Book 2
Dead Angels (Kiera Hudson Series 2) Book 3
Dead Statues (Kiera Hudson Series 2) Book 4
Dead Seth (Kiera Hudson Series 2) Book 5
Dead Wolf (Kiera Hudson Series 2) Book 6
Dead Water (Kiera Hudson Series 2) Book 7
Dead Push (Kiera Hudson Series 2) Book 8
Dead Lost (Kiera Hudson Series 2) Book 9
Dead End (Kiera Hudson Series 2) Book 10

Kiera Hudson Series Three
The Creeping Men (Kiera Hudson Series Three) Book 1
The Lethal Infected (Kiera Hudson Series Three) Book 2
The Adoring Artist (Kiera Hudson Series Three) Book 3
The Secret Identity (Kiera Hudson Series Three) Book 4
The White Wolf (Kiera Hudson Series Three) Book 5

Werewolves of Shade
Werewolves of Shade (Part One)
Werewolves of Shade (Part Two)

Werewolves of Shade (Part Three)
Werewolves of Shade (Part Four)
Werewolves of Shade (Part Five)
Werewolves of Shade (Part Six)

Moon Trilogy
Moonlight (Moon Trilogy) Book 1
Moonbeam (Moon Trilogy) Book 2
Moonshine (Moon Trilogy) Book 3

The Jack Seth Novellas
Hollow Pit (Book One)
Seeking Cara (Book Two) Coming Soon!

Black Hill Farm (Books 1 & 2)
Black Hill Farm (Book 1)
Black Hill Farm: Andy's Diary (Book 2)

Sydney Hart Novels
Witch (A Sydney Hart Novel) Book 1
Yellow (A Sydney Hart Novel) Book 2

The Doorways Saga
Doorways (Doorways Saga Book 1)
The League of Doorways (Doorways Saga Book 2)
The Queen of Doorways (Doorways Saga Book 3)

The Tessa Dark Trilogy
Stilts (Book 1)
Zip (Book 2)

The Mechanic

The Mechanic

The Dark Side of Nightfall
The Dark Side of Nightfall (Book One)
The Dark Side of Nightfall (Book Two)

Unscathed
Written by Tim O'Rourke & C.J. Pinard

Also by Tim O'Rourke writing as Jamie Drew
The November lake Mysteries
November Lake Teenage Detective (Book One)
November Lake Teenage Detective (Book Two)

You can contact Tim O'Rourke at
www.kierahudson.com or by email at kierahudson91@aol.com

Kiera Hudson & The White Wolf

Chapter One

Kiera

I watched Potter place the picture that Mavis Bateman had given him into his coat pocket. He looked over the stooped shoulders of the woman who stood before him. The fast fading sunlight illuminated the drying tears that ran the length of his ashen face. I took a deep breath, readying myself for the fit of rage I expected Potter to now fly into. But to my surprise, he did no such thing. Instead, he placed a cigarette into his mouth, lit it, then drew in deeply. Streams of grey-blue smoke flooded from his nostrils, forming a hazy cloud in the poky front room of Mavis Bateman's cottage. Any other old woman might have objected to the pungent smoke, but Mavis was a Lycanthrope. Did such smoke bother her aging lungs?

"What was written on the back of the photograph of your mother and Amity?" I asked, taking a step closer to Potter and gently placing one hand on his arm.

He continued to stare ahead out of the window and across the golden fields that stretched away into the distance. "Push," he whispered, as if his voice was coming from some far off place. Mavis eyed him as much as I.

"They found each other then," I said, gently squeezing Potter's arm. "That's a good thing, isn't it?" For the first time, I was struggling to find the right words – if there were any – to comfort the man I loved with all my heart. Were words even needed? He knew that I was here for him – I was by his side – always.

"I guess," Potter said, a thin line of smoke trailing upwards from the cigarette that jutted from the corner of his mouth.

Lowering her gaze, Mavis turned and using her walking frame for support, she shuffled back across the room. Once more she reached into the drawer where she had taken the picture of Joan and Amity from. I watched her close her claw-like fist around something and come slowly back toward us. "There's something else I would like to give you," she said, stooping once more before Potter and looking up into his pale face.

He cocked an eyebrow at her. "What?"

Slowly, Mavis uncurled her liver-spotted fist to reveal a ring. It was gold and shimmered in the fading sunlight that streamed in through the window and into the room. "My daughter, Amity, had planned on giving this to your mother, Joan. It was a sign of the unbreakable love Amity had for her. But of course – she didn't get the chance… you know the rest… there's no need to go over it all again. I want you to have it."

Potter looked down at the ring, then back at the old woman. "Why?"

"It was intended for your mother and you're her son," Mavis croaked. "I think it now belongs to you. This ring is a good thing, Potter. The ring represents love – it was bought by my daughter for that reason. It was a gift and now I'm giving it to you – I think your mother would be happy if she knew that you had it. After all, she loved you so much. You loved her, too."

Slowly, Potter reached out and closed his fingers around the ring that Mavis was offering him. "Thank you," he said, his voice barely a whisper. Without opening his fist to look at the ring, he placed it into his pocket, along with the photograph of his mother and Amity. A heavy silence fell over the room and once more, Potter turned to look out of the window, his profile bathed gold in the light from the sun. I could see that the tears had all dried away now. But his eyes were so very dark – so very black. I wondered what was going on behind them. I had never seen Potter look – look so empty. He looked like he'd had his guts kicked out of him. Potter had always been such a smart mouth. He had a snarky comment for every situation. But now he just stood silently and looked out of the window. I looked at Mavis. Our eyes locked and I sensed we were both thinking the same thing. Potter was hurting bad. He was probably hurting more than he ever had. I had known Potter to take a lot of beatings in his life – I'd even seen him have his heart ripped out. But that had been a physical thing. I think Potter knew how to deal with physical pain – those scars he seemed to be able to heal from quite quickly – but had Potter ever felt such emotional pain? Was this the first time in his life that he'd truly had his heartbroken? Discovering that his father had murdered his mother had seemed to leave him like some faint apparition of his former cocky self. But something else was different, too. Potter now had a wolf lurking deep inside of him. We both did. How would such a thing affect him? Potter already struggled with his anger from time to time just like my brother, Jack, had. It was at discovering that his mother – Kathy Seth – had killed his sisters that Jack finally let the wolf consume him. It was the pain and anguish at losing his sisters and discovering his mother's betrayal that the wolf struck and literally sunk its claws into my brother's heart. Would the wolf now living inside of Potter seize this moment to take him like it had taken my brother? I didn't want that for Potter. It was no way to live. To be consumed by hate would only destroy the man I loved like it had destroyed Jack. That would poison him, make him vulnerable to the wolf – leave his soul unguarded and free to be taken. Would the hate for his father make Potter wither and age with anger and loathing like it had Jack? I couldn't bear to watch such a thing happen. I wouldn't let the wolf destroy Potter, like it had my half-brother.

"You look as if you're both fit to drop," Mavis said with a weak smile. "I don't have much, but I could make you both supper."

"I'm not hungry," Potter said. He took the smouldering cigarette end from the corner of his mouth, pushed open the window, and tossed it out into the flowerbed.

"Some rest then," Mavis said. "You both look as if you haven't had a good night's sleep in weeks."

I recalled the nights I had sat in the outhouse watching Potter as he'd wrestled with the wolf inside of him. Was he still fighting it? He looked not to be. He looked calm – too calm – like a darkening sea before a storm. Perhaps some rest would do him good – the both of us some good.

I smiled back at Mavis. "You're very kind."

"I have a spare room and bed that you could share," Mavis said.

Without looking at her, Potter said over his shoulder, "Was it your daughter's – Amity's room? Did she share it with my mother?"

"Yes, but not in this layer," Mavis said.

"That was their place…." Potter started.

"The barn then," I cut in. "Where Nev used to live. There's a bed… we could rest in there…"

"Who's Nev?" Potter asked, glancing back over his shoulder at me.

I looked at Potter. "Nev was a friend."

"You've never mentioned him before," Potter said.

"He was someone I met in this layer," I said, glancing at Mavis then back at Potter who had now turned his back on the window and had me trapped in his dark stare.

"Where is this Nev now?" he asked me.

Again I looked at Mavis. I hadn't had the heart to tell her that the young man who had once been so kind to her had been beaten to death by the wolves that had set up camp in the valley. I had simply told her that he wouldn't ever be coming back.

"Like your mother, Nev's gone to another layer." I glanced at Mavis and she met me with her milky stare. She nodded her head slowly and I sensed she knew what I meant by that.

"Will the war never end?" she tutted, heading back to her threadbare armchair by the window. She eased herself down into it, her knee joints making a cracking sound.

"The war?" I asked her.

"The war between the Vampyrus and Lycanthrope," she said, the last of the sunlight trapped in her wispy white hair. "Haven't enough of us died already? Can't a peace be found?"

Potter glanced down at her and she back at him.

"I guess peace will never be found while war rages in our own hearts," she said, as if searching his dark eyes with her own. "But a heart that knows peace knows true love and that is the most precious of all things. I've only ever seen it twice in my life."

"Where?" Potter asked her.

"In Amity's eyes when she looked at your mother," Mavis said with a wistful smile as if remembering her daughter's face.

"And the second time?" Potter said.

"I see that same look in Kiera's eyes," Mavis said. "I see it every time she looks at you, Potter."

He looked at me, then back at the old woman sitting hunched forward in the chair. Her eyes suddenly sparkled as if the last shafts of daylight had been soaked up by them. "Don't let your hate destroy your love, Potter, like your father's hate destroyed the love my daughter and your mother shared. The world – the layers – the *wheres* and *whens* – the Lycanthrope and Vampyrus need every last ounce of love if any of us have a chance of surviving."

"You sound like my mother," Potter almost seemed to scoff in that way he always did.

"And if I was your mother, I'd tell you to take Kiera, who I can see loves you so much, and run and run and run from this place and never look back. I'd tell you to go away and live your lives – treasure every moment you have with her – but something tells me that such a thing isn't possible – it isn't possible for either of you."

"Why not?" I asked.

"Because one of your hearts is filled with hate," she said, holding her stare on Potter. "A heart that is filled with hate never knows true love."

Potter looked at me, then back at Mavis.

As if being able to see into Potter's heart, Mavis added, "Don't hate your father for what he did."

"Why not?" Potter asked.

"Because then he has killed you, too," Mavis said. "He's dragged you into that fire like he dragged your mother that night."

"This just sounds like a bunch of bullshit if you ask me," Potter said. "People that don't *push* back are weak."

Mavis half smiled back at him. "Is it bullshit? Doesn't your hate and anger for your father burn? Doesn't your heart feel as if it's on fire? Doesn't your rage feel like a seething inferno...?"

"Where's this barn? I don't need a shrink – I need some rest," Potter said, stepping away from the window. He brushed past me as he headed for the door.

"Don't let it consume you, Potter," Mavis said, before Potter disappeared around the edge of the door and out of the room.

I heard the front door swing open, then slam shut. Once

the sound of the front door rattling in its frame had diminished, I looked across the room at the frail woman. "Thank you," I said.

"For what, dear?"

"For trying to talk some sense into Potter." I told her. "I don't know if it will work, but you were right about one thing."

"And what was that?" she turned her head on her withered neck to look at me.

"I know he can be a real jerk at times, and you're right, he is full of hate and I'm scared that what he's learnt about his father will make that anger worse, but I do love him. I love Potter more than I've ever loved anyone," I said.

With that spark fading in her eyes, Mavis said, "But will your love for him be enough to save him… save him from the wolf I can see staring back at me from the darkness that clouds his eyes?"

Chapter Two

Potter

You were right – that old hag was talking bullshit, the wolf whispered from deep inside of me. Its voice floated up out of the darkness like that of someone who had just woken to find themselves buried alive in a grave. The voice sounded scared – frantic somehow. Did it fear that I might just listen and see some sense in what the old woman had said?

"You can shut the fuck up, too," I spoke out loud as if talking to myself, but hoping the wolf would hear me. It was almost full dark now and the first of the stars could be seen in the breaks amongst the clouds that lumbered overhead.

Oh, c'mon, Seany-porny, you don't really believe all that horseshit, do you? the wolf teased, the fear I thought I'd heard in its voice no longer present.

"Don't call me that," I snapped back. "My name is Potter."

I was just yanking on your chain that was all, don't be so fucking prickly the whole time. We're friends now...

"We're not friends," I said as the wind that gusted across the open fields made the front door of the cottage rattle in its frame. I took several steps down the path, fearing that if Kiera or Mavis heard me talking to the wolf they might think I'd lost my mind. "You're a wolf and I fucking hate you," I mumbled under my breath, dropping my head low as if talking into my chest.

It's not me you should hate, the wolf chuckled. *It wasn't me that killed your mother – it was your father – a Vampyrus. It's the Vampyrus you should hate, not the wolves...*

"Screw you," I said, letting my wings suddenly tear from my back and claws from my fists.

"Going somewhere?" I heard someone ask.

I spun around to find Kiera standing in the open doorway. Mavis was right, she did look deadbeat. I had never seen her skin look so pale – it was almost paper white. Her long black hair that was streaked with blue hung limply about her shoulders. It no longer gleamed like it once had. Her hazel eyes looked flat, like they too had lost their spark. But yet, Kiera still looked more beautiful than any woman I had ever seen or could imagine as she stood in the open doorway of the cottage.

"I'm not going anywhere," I said, fighting the urge to race toward her, swoop her up in my arms, and hold her tight to me.

"Then why are your wings out?" she asked, closing the door behind her and coming along the path toward me.

"I dunno," I shrugged. Why had I released my wings and claws? Had it been to make me feel more Vampyrus than wolf? Had I hoped the sound of my beating wings would drown out the sound of the wolf's voice? If it had been, then it seemed to have done the trick. I could no longer hear the wolf's voice – for now at least. It was like it had skulked away inside of me – *pushed* back into the darkness of my soul by the Vampyrus.

Reaching me, Kiera took my hands in hers. Her skin felt ice cold. She looked into my eyes as if reading me – *seeing* me for the first time. "You're still fighting the wolf, aren't you?" she whispered.

"I've been fighting the wolves my whole life," I told her.

"Then perhaps it's time to stop," Kiera said, her eyes never leaving mine.

"But I'm frightened," I confessed to her. "I'm frightened of what I might become if I let the wolf come forward – let it become a part of me."

"If we love what scares us then can we ever fear it again?" Kiera said. "Can it ever truly have a hold over us?"

"Are you happy that you're half wolf?" I asked.

"Not at first," Kiera said, leading me slowly by the hand away from the cottage and toward a barn in a nearby field. "It wasn't easy for me to learn that I was a half and half – that my brother was the serial killer, Jack Seth. I didn't want to be a wolf any more than you do now..."

"But I didn't ask for it..." I cut in.

"And neither did I," Kiera said, glancing sideways at me as her hair blew about the sides of her ashen face. "But you know, Mavis is right. I could have carried on fighting the wolf, pretending it wasn't there – running from it. But I was only running from myself. It didn't matter how hard and fast I ran, every time I looked in the mirror it was there – the wolf was staring back at me – it always caught up with me. It was the same on learning that I was a half Vampyrus. I hated the thought of it living inside of me – those little bony black claws at the tips of each wing hiding inside of me. But what good did hating them bring? I only hated myself. For hours I would stand naked in front of the mirror at Hallowed Manor and stare back at my reflection. Sometimes I would be in my Vampyrus form, and then other times as a human. But what I learnt, was that although they looked different, they were one in the same, both parts were me, both were an equal part – they made me what I am – who I am. Just like the wolf is a part of me. There is nothing I can do to change that. So do I spend the rest of my life hating myself – just to escape from myself? Or do I try and love the *who* and *what* I am? Doesn't it make more sense for me to try and be the best that I can be – whatever I truly am?"

"But I'm not like you, Kiera," I said as we reached the barn. She pushed the door open and led me inside. There was an easel in the middle of the room and some paintings propped against the wall. In the far corner I could see a bed. Kiera closed the door behind us, sealing us in near darkness. I sought out her hands and took hold of them. "I don't see things the way you do," I told her.

"In the darkness all of us are the same," she whispered, seeking out my lips. I felt them brush over mine. "It is only the light that highlights our differences – illuminates our imperfections."

I whispered into her ear as I slid her coat off where it dropped to the floor. "I wasn't aware that you had any imperfections." I pulled her shirt off and ran my claws over her soft but cold flesh. "You feel perfect to me." Working blind, I unfastened her bra and let if fall to the floor as Kiera pushed open my coat, revealing my bare chest beneath. I pulled her close, our bodies pressed against each other. It felt like an eternity since we had been together like this. I folded my wings tight about us as if ensnaring her – never wanting to let her go.

I felt Kiera's hands fumble with my belt buckle as I slid her jeans down over her hips. Still wrapped in my wings and standing naked together, I felt Kiera's own wings open. They felt like sheets made of the finest silk as I brushed my hands over them. How could Kiera have ever been scared or repulsed by them? They were beautiful – she was beautiful – in the darkness or the light.

"I love you," I whispered, holding her tight in my arms.

"I love you more," she whispered back before leading me across the barn to the bed.

Chapter Three

Kiera

To be as one with Potter again felt incredible. Not purely because of the intense feelings of pleasure that now washed through and over me, but because I was close to him again. I felt safe in his arms and I knew that we belonged together. It was like having him inside of me wasn't enough. I wanted to get lost in him somehow and he in me. With Potter moving his strong hips slowly back and forth, I wrapped my legs tight about him, throwing my arms around his back. I pulled Potter deeper into me as he lost his hands in my hair. We smothered each other with kisses as we lay entwined upon the bed. Thoughts of pushing him away on the underground station flooded my mind and I felt a spike of pain. I never wanted to be apart from him again. I never wanted to let go of him. I didn't ever want to live without the intense feelings he now stirred in me as we made love on the bed. How had I ever let him go? How had I ever believed that I could be happy without him? It wasn't just the extreme physical love that I had missed being apart from Potter – there was more to it than that. I had missed his companionship, his friendship, and knowing that he was there for me. There had been the other Potter, but he hadn't been mine – not really. He had belonged to another. The Potter in this layer had belonged to Sophie despite the feelings that he said he'd had for me. He had only been a shadow of the man that I truly loved. But that Potter was dead now – I had killed him. The wolf that I had now accepted as part of me had ripped out his throat. Had I had any right to kill him any more than I would've had the right to take him as my lover? He was with Sophie – they were having a child together. My brother, Jack, had come to me in my dreams. He had told me that Potter and I had a daughter – Jack had met her in the layer he had been *pushed* into. I believed that Jack had been talking about the child Sophie and the Potter from this layer were having. But had Jack been right after all? I hadn't foreseen my Potter coming to join me in this layer. I had believed that my Potter had been lost to me – that I had *pushed* him and my friends away forever. So did Potter and I now have a daughter at some point in the future? We were meant to be married after all. Was I somehow getting a second shot at being happy? Was I being rewarded in some way? And if so, why? And who was it that believed I deserved to have Potter back in my life? Who believed that I deserved such happiness and joy? Noah? Whoever, and for whatever reason – I planned not to lose Potter from my life again. Only death would separate us, and even then I would haunt him given half the chance.

    With thoughts of losing Potter again swirling like a dense fog at the corners of my mind, I screwed my eyes shut and pulled Potter closer still in my arms. Working our hips together in unison, I tilted my head back and let Potter caress my neck as his lips brushed over the soft flesh there. I felt the rough prickle of his stubble then something else – something sharper pierced my flesh. I felt Potter's fangs sink into my neck, then the heady rush of something close to ecstasy as he sucked my blood into his mouth. The physical act of lovemaking and becoming one was only made more intense by sharing each other's blood. With the side of his face against mine, I nipped the flesh at the base of his neck with my fangs. I felt the first drops of his blood against my lips. I licked them greedily away with the tip of my tongue. The taste of his red stuff was like an explosion in my mouth. It tasted sweet – like the most perfect wine. Now that I had tasted it again after such a long time, my very being cried out for more. Every single pore seemed to open, ready to soak up his life's blood. With a blissful urgency now raging hot deep inside of me, I sunk my fangs deep into his neck and let his blood gush into my mouth. Every one of my nerve endings sparked with pleasure as Potter worked faster and faster above me, driving his hips back and forth as we fed on each other's love and blood. Wrapping my legs tighter about his back, I sunk my claws into his tight arse and dragged him deeper into me, wanting all of him – everything he could give me. When his own pleasure became all consuming, Potter pulled his fangs from my neck and arching his back, he threw his head backwards. With my eyes half open, I peered up through my lashes at him. I could see a trail of my own blood leaking from the corner of his mouth. Potter had his own eyes screwed shut, his face a mask of agonising pleasure as he rocked back and forth at an ever increasing speed above me. Arching my back from off the bed, I matched his speed as I gyrated my hips beneath him. My lips felt sticky with his blood. Reaching out with one hand and gripping the sheets with the other, I lost my fingers in his hair and dragged his face down toward mine. I kissed him, my excitement only growing ever more feverish as I could taste my own blood on his lips. He swirled his tongue around the inside of my mouth our pleasure reaching its peak for the both of us. Breaking our kiss, Potter threw back his head and cried out, his whole body shaking and trembling above me as he bucked back and forth in my arms.

"I love…" but before I'd had the chance to finish, the last of my words was snatched away as my own body gave into the crippling feeling of pleasure that now consumed my body. I shook and trembled violently beneath Potter – those feelings of desire that now filled my body almost agony in their intensity.

And even as those feelings started to weaken and spread

their joy as far as my fingers and toes, we stayed joined as one. Gasping for breath, Potter collapsed in my arms. His unkempt hair was damp and felt soft against my breasts as my chest hitched up and down. With every muscle in my body now growing soft and malleable, I unlocked my legs and arms from around Potter. With my flesh still tingling with joy, Potter rolled from off me and onto his side. Cupping one of my breasts in his hands and sliding the other about my waist, he pulled me close next him. Although my skin felt hot, the room was cold, so I let my wings fall over us like the softest of blankets.

    With our noses almost touching, I looked back into Potter's black eyes. "I love you, Potter," I whispered, still trying to find my breath.

    "Then why did you leave?" he asked. "Why did you *push* me away on that underground platform? You broke my fucking heart, Kiera."

Chapter Four

Kiera

I rolled onto my back and stared up at the ceiling of the barn. It was dark, but I could still see the ancient beams that crisscrossed overhead, which kept the rickety roof from being blown away in the growing wind that whined like some petulant child outside. What did I say to Potter? How did I even begin to explain why I had *pushed* him and my friends away?

Before I'd had a chance to gather my thoughts, Potter said, "You didn't have to push me away, Kiera. I would have gone anywhere with you. We were meant to have been getting married, remember?"

His breath was warm against my skin as he spoke and the sweet smell of blood wafted on it. Taking a deep breath, and turning my head to face him through the gloom, I said, "The Elders showed me these statues once. It seems like such a very long time ago now, but it was in the world that I *pushed* you, Murphy, and the others from. It was after leaving you to go in search of my father – before Jack held me hostage in that house at the top of the hill – where the church and the graveyard stood. It was in that graveyard that the Elders appeared to me. I felt lost and disorientated. I had been in desperate need of some Lot 13. I was cracking up – literally. I could see statues in the distance so I made my way toward them."

"What were these statues?" Potter asked, reaching down from the bed with one hand and blindly searching the floor. He didn't take his eyes from me once, like he feared I might just disappear from his life again. But I wasn't going to – not this time. I reached out and gently stroked the curve of his jaw. "Who did the statues look like?" he asked, pulling his discarded jeans from the floor and fishing a packet of cigarettes and lighter from the pocket. He lit one.

"The statues were my friends – you, Murphy, Kayla, Isidor," I explained. "All of you looked so happy – the happiest I'd ever seen any of you. But you only looked so happy because you were all with people you loved. Murphy was with his daughters, Kayla was with Sam, Isidor with Melody Rose, and you – you, Potter, were with Sophie."

"But…" Potter put in.

"Listen," I said, placing one finger gently against his lips. "The Elders told me that I had to make a choice. I had to make a choice between saving the humans or the Vampyrus. If I did that, then you and the others would all be *pushed* back to lives where you would be happy."

"What about you?" Potter asked, blowing smoke from the corner of his mouth where it drifted up toward the ceiling. "If you chose, would you get *pushed* back, too?"

I shook my head. "No. I couldn't go back any more than I could choose between the humans and the Vampyrus. So if what the Elders said was true, none of you would have been happy again. All of you would have been stuck in that layer – your lives little more than pure misery and I would have had to watch you suffer knowing that I couldn't have put things right. I couldn't bear to watch the people I loved the most suffer because of me, so I was desperate to find another way. It seemed like the Elders with their ancient and stitched together faces held all the cards. But then I found Noah – or perhaps he found me. It was he who told me that the Elders were nothing more than leaches who fed off – grew strong and stayed alive – by feeding off my misery. The

Elders knew that they had put me in an impossible situation – had conjured a trap that I couldn't escape from. They knew that if I chose to destroy either the humans or the Vampyrus, the guilt would have haunted me forevermore – an agonising guilt that they would have fed off. But if I chose to do nothing, then you would have all been trapped in that layer and I would have had to spend the rest of my life watching you all suffer knowing that you could be happy in some other *where* and *when*. Once again, the Elders would have fed off my misery and guilt. It was Noah, as we sat and talked in that shifting Grand Railway Station between the layers, who told me that I wasn't *seeing* the way out of the trap that the Elders had set for me. My anguish had made me blind to it. I had lost sight of the fact that I loved you – loved all my friends so much – that some part of me would have been happy knowing that none of you were suffering anymore. Why wouldn't I have been happy in the knowledge that you were all with the people that you loved? How could I have been so selfish? And as I sat and talked it through with Noah on the concourse of that Grand Station, I felt something I hadn't felt in a very long time. I felt a spark of happiness. I remembered those statues the Elders had shown me. I could see how happy you all looked - how your smiles beamed. And it was then I realised that I was doing something I hadn't done in a very long time – since being *pushed* into that godforsaken layer – I was smiling too. I was smiling at the thought of you all being happy. Why wouldn't I have wanted such a thing for the people I loved more than anyone or anything in the world?"

"But how could you ever believe that any of us would have been happy without you in our lives, Kiera?" Potter frowned. He extinguished the smouldering cigarette end between his finger and thumb. "Did you think we would just forget all about you?"

"That was the whole point," I tried to explain. "None of

you were ever meant to remember me. It was meant to have been as if I had never existed to you. You can't miss what you've never known."

"Well I did remember," Potter scowled. "How could I forget when the first thing I see after being *pushed* from the Grand Station was a giant fucking statue of you! There you were – made of stone – naked with wings and tits hanging out! How did you ever think I could forget you?"

"Something must have gone wrong…" I cut in.

"Yeah, that fuck-wit, Noah, got it wrong," Potter said, rolling onto his back and sighing. He lit another cigarette. "Who is he anyway – this Noah bloke? Who put him in charge?"

"He was an Elder once."

"Oh great," Potter said, jetting thick streams of smoke from his nostrils.

"He isn't like the others," I explained. "The other Elders banished him to that railway station."

"I'd like to do more than banish him - I'd like to kick his fucking arse for coming up with such a stupid idea…" Potter started.

"It was my choice," I said. "Don't you see that? And it was the only choice I had if I was going to save you and my friends."

A silence hung in the air only broken by the wind crying outside.

"So where are the Elders now?" Potter finally asked.

"When they realised that I had tricked them – when they realised that they had underestimated my love for my friends and that I could be happy without them as long as I knew you were all happy, the Elders turned to nothing but dust and were sucked into the darkness of the tunnel that led from the underground platform."

"So are they dead? Have we seen the last of the evil

fuckers?" Potter asked, glancing at me.

"I think so," I said. "My life here hasn't been a bed of roses recently and I haven't seen or heard of the Elders. I look for cracks now and then – you know, on my skin and up in the sky, but I haven't seen any."

"So what happened to you after you tricked – after you *pushed* us all away that day?" Potter asked.

I sensed a flicker of resentment in Potter's voice for what I had done – and could I really blame him for feeling the way he did? Wouldn't I be feeling exactly the same if he had *pushed* me away? It would have broken my heart. Taking a deep breath, I said, "I boarded the next train from that station. The train entered the tunnel and the next thing I knew I was in my car driving along the coastal road toward the Raged Cove. At first I thought I'd ended up back where I had started – heading back into the cove to take up my post as police recruit. But everything was different."

"Like what?"

I half smiled. "Well, the sun was shining to start with. I don't think I can remember a day when the sun had shone in the Ragged Cove the first time around. But there was other stuff too – like I wasn't dressed as a cop. I wore a tight pencil skirt and heels…"

Potter smirked. "I would've quite liked to have seen that. I don't s'pose you still have those high heels, do you?"

"Why, do you want to borrow them?"

"That wasn't exactly what I had in mind," he said right back. "I was thinking that perhaps you might want to wear them the next time we…"

I spoke over him. "It wasn't just the weather or how I was dressed that was different this time around. Apparently I worked for some kind of temping agency and I had been sent to the

Ragged Cove to be some kind of secretary…"

"High heels! Saucy-secretary! Christ, I really have been missing all the action!" Potter said with a wicked grin and a look of devilment in his eyes.

"But you didn't miss out," I said, trying to remain serious.

"What do you mean by that?"

"There is – there *was* – another Potter, another you in this layer," I explained.

Potter looked at me, his eyes two black wells. "When I was sick – when I was struggling with the wolf and you had me chained up, I can remember you saying something about me and Sophie."

"The Potter in this layer was getting married to her," I told him.

"Was?" Potter frowned. "You keep saying *was*. Where is this other version of me now?"

"I killed him."

Chapter Five

Kiera

"*You* killed him!" Potter said, sitting bolt upright. He took another cigarette from the pack and popped it into the corner of his mouth where he stroked the tip of it with a flame from his lighter. "What is this? You get shot of me by *pushing* me onto a train and then you murder me..."

"It wasn't you that I killed," I insisted. "And besides it wasn't really me who killed you – killed the *other* Potter. It was the wolf that did that."

"Did you bang this other Potter?" he asked, shooting me a quick look.

I gasped at what he'd just asked me, my mouth dropping open. "Bang him?"

"Yeah, you know – jiggy-jiggy?"

"No, I did not," I said, feeling affronted by his question. "Is that all you're worried about?"

"It's just that this Potter would've looked like me – he was me..."

"He wasn't you – he was engaged to Sophie Harrison – not me. Do you really think I could sleep with another woman's man?"

"But..."

"No buts, Potter," I said. "I'm not like that. I admit it might have been difficult for me to be around him, as he was so much like you, but..."

"But you killed him," Potter reminded me.

"I told you that it was the wolf that did that," I said, looking away. "You know I'm a half and half. The wolf came forward inside of me in this layer just like the wolf has come forward in you. But what I don't understand is why you now have a wolf living in you – you're not a half and half like me. Neither of your parents were Lycanthrope like my true mother, Kathy Seth."

Sitting up in bed with his back flat against the wall of the barn, Potter drew deeply on the cigarette that dangled from the corner of his mouth. The end winked on and off in the dark like a slow blinking eye. "After you *pushed* us, Murphy and the rest of us found ourselves in Snake Weed, where there is that statue of you – where I saw you looking back at me in the water at the foot of the fountain. I knew that you were still alive. We might not have been in the same layer, but you were out there. And despite the bullshit that old-git, Noah, obviously fed you, I still remembered you. We all did. The fact that I could see you in the water suggested that there were still some cracks open. There is only one person I know who truly understands the cracks and the layers and that's Lilly Blu. I asked her to help me to pass through them so I could get to you. Lilly refused at first. She said that it was dangerous and that once I had passed into another layer I might not ever get back to Murphy and the others. But it was a risk I was prepared to take – it was a risk that I did take so that I could be with you again, Kiera."

Learning what Potter had risked to find me, I reached out and closed my hand around his. He gently squeezed my fingers with his. But he didn't meet my stare, he sat looking straight ahead and into the darkness.

Potter continued. "Lilly led me away from Murphy and the others and into some remote valley. At the far end of it stood some old shack. She told me to go inside. As she shut the door on me she said that I might not like what I find on the other side –

what I might change into. I pushed open the door to ask her what she meant by that, but she no longer stood on the other side of that doorway – it was you I could see, Kiera. Until now, I don't remember much else other than fighting the wolf that had somehow crept inside of me. And it's now that I realise what Lilly Blu meant when she said I might not like what I find – what I might change into in this layer. Why didn't she tell me? But then again, I'm not sure that she even really wanted to. Why would she have? Lilly Blu is only on one side, and that is her own."

"Would it have made any difference even if she had?" I asked him. "If Lilly Blu had told you that there was a risk that you might have changed into a wolf, would you have still come in search of me?"

He cocked an eyebrow at me. "Do you really need to ask me that?"

"I guess not," I said looking down.

"But why a wolf?" Potter asked, more himself than me. "Why is there now a wolf living inside of me?"

"That valley means something to the wolves," I said. "It's some kind of sacred ground. That shack is a part of it. Apparently it holds some kind of special significance to the Lycanthrope in this layer."

"How do you know that?"

"You told me." I shook my head. "What I mean is – the other Potter told me."

"Apart from being engaged to Sophie, what was this other Potter like?" he asked. "Is Murphy in this layer too?"

"He is," I explained. "Potter and Murphy were part of an organisation called The Creeping Men."

"What, they were both pervs or something?"

"No, they weren't perverts, but they are different from you and the Murphy that we know and love. Mrs. Payne is here too..."

"That old cow," Potter chipped in.

"And she's got the hots for Murphy," I grinned. "She keeps trying to give him a bed bath."

"And I thought you said that Murphy wasn't a perv in this layer," Potter smiled back at me. "What about Kayla and Shaggy-Doo?"

"If you mean Kayla and Isidor, they are here, but as of yet I haven't met or seen them."

"Why not?"

"It's like they've gone missing," I said. "Every time I ask about them, people clam up."

"Like who?" Potter frowned.

"Ravenwood, for one."

"Jeez, he's here, too?" Potter said, crushing out the cigarette and lighting another almost at once. "It's like some kind of college reunion. Perhaps I should talk to him."

"You can't."

"Why not?"

"Ravenwood's dead," I said. "Sophie killed him."

"Sophie killed him?" Potter said, his brow creasing. "What did the old sod ever do to her?"

"He tried to poison her," I explained.

"Poison her!" Potter said, spluttering up a lungful of smoke. "So let me get this right. You killed me, Ravenwood tried to murder Sophie, so she in return killed him. Jesus, this sounds like a Miss Marple novel written by Agatha Christie while she was out of her skull on crack."

"It gets worse," I said, looking at him.

"What? Don't tell me, that old fart Murphy has gone and got old Mother Hubbard Mrs. Payne pregnant," Potter scoffed.

"Not exactly," I said.

"How exactly?"

I took a deep breath before talking again. "You got Sophie pregnant. She's carrying your baby in this layer."

"Not my baby," Potter said, shooting to his feet. "Not in this layer – not *ever*."

I reached for him, taking his hand and pulling him back down onto the bed. He sat beside me, eyes never leaving mine. "It's not just the baby. You turned Sophie – you changed her into a vampire."

"But if a Vampyrus bites a human they turn weird – like zombies," Potter said.

"Not in this layer," I told him. "Sophie was given some kind of potion called Lot 12..."

"Don't you mean Lot 13?"

Then looking at each other, we both said at once, "Not in this layer."

"Ravenwood switched the potion with poison," I said.

"But why would he have wanted to kill her?"

"Ravenwood died before I had a chance to find out," I explained. "But that's not all, when I returned to his body to bury him, he was gone."

"So Ravenwood could still be alive? Potter asked.

"Or someone stole his corpse away."

Potter sat thoughtfully for a moment, dragging smoke down into his lungs and let it ooze from his nose and the corners of his mouth. Just when I thought I might lose sight of him in the cloud that was fast forming, he looked at me and said, "Where's Sophie now?"

"She's recovering in that makeshift hospital in the roof of Hallowed Manor." I said. "Murphy is there, too."

"I have to go and see him," Potter said. Crushing out the cigarette and standing up again. He picked up his jeans from off the floor and pulled them up over his legs.

"He's not our Murphy," I said, climbing from the edge of the bed and scooping up my own clothes.

"Once an old fart always an old fart," Potter said, zipping up the front of his jeans with one quick tug.

"Listen to me," I said, taking hold of Potter's arm. "Murphy isn't your friend. He's different here."

"What – he's ditched those old slippers?" Potter chuckled to himself while pulling on his long dark coat.

"He murdered Lilly Blu," I said.

Potter gawped at me, mouth open. "I wasn't kidding about that fucked up Miss Marple book. "What about Meren and Nes..."

"Murphy doesn't have any daughters in this layer. As far as I know they don't exist and Murphy hasn't ever heard of them," I explained. "And that's not the only thing they don't know exists."

"What else?" Potter shot at me.

"Murphy – the others – none of them seem to know anything about The Hollows. As far as they're concerned there is no such place."

"But it's our home – where we come from," Potter said.

"It's not their home – not here."

"So what do we do now?" He sounded exasperated. "We're both stuck here – we're both wolves, my best mate has killed his wife and started having jiggy-jiggy with the old maid..."

"We need to find Lilly Blu," I cut in.

"I thought you said she was dead."

"There is a white wolf," I started to explain, pulling on my coat and turning up the collar. "After I killed you in this layer, the white wolf led me through that valley and to that old shack. While the white wolf watched I placed the dead body of that other Potter inside and closed the door. It was then as I sat in that valley with the white wolf that you appeared from inside that shack.

Don't you see that it was the same valley and the same shack, just in different layers? That's all. Just as Lilly Blu led me to the shack in this layer, she led you to it in another. She brought us back together."

"What makes you think that this white wolf is Lilly Blu?" Potter asked.

"Murphy killed Lilly Blu in this layer because he discovered that she was a Lycanthrope," I said. "Murphy cut off her head and then scattered her remains on un-sacred ground. Since that time a white wolf has been seen in that valley. The Lycanthrope believe it to be the spirit of Lilly Blu."

"Why would they think that?"

"Because Lilly Blu was the Queen of the Lycanthrope in this *where* and *when*."

"And who told you all of this?" Potter asked me.

"You did," I said, before heading for the barn door.

"Hey," Potter called after me.

With one hand on the barn door handle, I glanced back over my shoulder at him as he came toward me. "Huh?"

"If Ravenwood poisoned Sophie, how come she is still alive?" Potter asked.

"Because I saved her," I told him, pulling open the door and stepping out into the night.

Chapter Six

Potter

"Why would you want to save *her*?" I asked, the barn door nearly hitting me in the arse as I headed after Kiera into the night. "I thought you were jealous as hell where Sophie was concerned."

"Me, jealous?" Kiera said, spinning around on the heel of her boots to face me. She clawed long lengths of black and blue hair from in front of her eyes so I could see them. Did she want me to be able to see her unflinching stare? "Have I got anything to be jealous about?" she asked me. Did she still feel the pain that she had once felt when discovering I had once left her and Hallowed Manor to go in search of Sophie? But I had only done that to try and find out what the new world that we had been *pushed* into was like. There had been no other reason than that.

"Of course you have nothing to be jealous about," I assured her.

"Then why wouldn't I have saved her?" Kiera said, that hazel spark back in her eyes, hands on hips. Now that was the Kiera I knew and loved. "And besides, she was pregnant…"

"Was that the only reason?"

"Isn't that reason enough?" she came back at me. "Do you really think I would've let Sophie die even if I was jealous of her? Do you think I'm capable of doing such a thing?"

"No," I said with a shake of my head. I took a step closer to her – close enough that I could take one of her cold hands in mine. I folded my fingers over hers, brought them up to my mouth, and kissed them. "A lot of women would have been happy to have seen Sophie suffer."

"But I'm not like that," she said, sliding her hand from mine.

I watched her turn once more and head down the path that led around the side of the cottage. All the windows were in darkness and I guessed that Mavis Bateman had gone to bed for the night. How late was it, exactly? I had no idea. The moon was high up in the sky and made to look crescent shaped by a passing cloud. The night was star-shot and for the first time since waking in that room to find myself chained to the bed, I felt a certain kind of peace. The wolf was silent. For now.

Ahead of me, Kiera swung open the garden gate and stepped out onto the remote country road that twisted away in either direction. Jogging to catch up with her, I stopped at the gate and said, "Where are you going?"

"Back to the valley – I think we should go in search of the white wolf."

"I'm not so sure," I said. "We don't even know if this white wolf really is Lilly Blu. And even if it is, how do we know we can trust her in this layer? Murphy wouldn't have killed her for nothing."

"Like I've already said, the Murphy in this *where* and *when* is different – he's not our Murphy. How do we know we can trust him? He killed Lilly Blu because he found out she was a wolf..."

"So?" I shrugged.

Kiera looked suddenly exasperated. "We're both wolves now! We're his enemy in this layer, not his friend."

"Listen, sweet-cheeks..."

"Don't call me that..."

"Okay, tiger."

"Nor that. Why do you have to be so difficult?" Kiera asked.

"You wouldn't have me any other way," I grinned back at her. She secretly liked it when I teased her. I knew. She knew it. That's how we rolled – picking at each other – but loving each other at the same time. It had always been the same between us and I guessed it would never change. I wasn't sure that I wanted it to. I liked getting under her skin. I loved it when she scowled at me. Christ, she looked hot when she did.

"All I'm saying is that we can't risk Murphy and any of the others discovering that we're wolves – that you're not the real Potter."

"I'm the real deal," I said, puffing out my chest at her.

"Not to the others you're not."

"What others? From what you've told me, I'm surprised there is anyone else left alive. It's like the murder capital of the world around here," I said, half joking but trying to make a serious point too. "I think we should go to Hallowed Manor and speak with Murphy."

"And say what?" Kiera said, setting off down the road in the dark.

"Find out why he really killed Lilly Blu," I said, setting off after her.

"But the Potter in this world might have already known that. Why would you be asking such a thing?"

"I'll play dumb."

"That shouldn't be too hard for you."

"I heard that."

Kiera half smiled at me. "You were meant to."

"Look, Kiera, I think that before we go off in search of the facts..."

"Facts!" Kiera almost seemed to scoff with disbelief. "When have you ever been interested in the facts? You usually let your claws do the talking first before you start asking questions."

"Well, yeah, but perhaps I've changed – perhaps I've learnt by my mistakes."

"Perhaps you've grown up." Kiera winked at me.

"Cheeky cow," I said with a half-smile. "Perhaps I just want to see that old fart Murphy get molested by old Mrs. Payne."

"That's not funny, Potter," Kiera said, her bright eyes growing wide. "I think he is actually scared of her."

"And that's why I can't believe Murphy – our Murphy or not – killed Lilly Blu without good reason," I said. "And we need to find out what that reason is before we go in search of this white wolf you talk of."

"Okay, okay," Kiera sighed. "Perhaps you're right. But you've got to promise me – no fighting, ripping, shredding, or biting."

"Not even a little?"

"Not a drop of blood is to be spilt tonight, Potter, there has been enough bloodshed already," Kiera warned me.

"I promise," I said.

"I'll come as far as the summerhouse with you that sits in the grounds of Hallowed Manor. I'll wait for you there," Kiera said.

"Why?" I asked.

"Because you're not the Potter from this layer – I killed him, remember?" Kiera explained. "We were different together. Being with him wasn't like being with you. Murphy might notice something out of place if he sees us both together. You might think that Murphy is some old fart but he's as sharp as any of us – if not sharper. Besides – there is something I have to do while you go and speak with Murphy."

"And what's that?" I watched Kiera reach into her coat pocket. She pulled out a small key.

"Where did you get that?" I asked her.

"Ravenwood gave it to me before he died," she said, closing her fist around it. "I'm going to see if I can find whatever it is the key opens."

"And where will you even know to look? Hallowed Manor is huge."

"Ravenwood said something before he died," Kiera said, placing the key back into her coat pocket. "He said he could hear the wind in the willows."

"There's those willow trees in the grounds of the manor – near to those graves," I reminded her.

"It was beneath those willow trees that Ravenwood died."

"Perhaps he really could just hear the wind in the trees, then?" I said.

"Perhaps," Kiera said. I could tell she wasn't convinced by my suggestion. Then looking at me, she said, "I'm glad you came after me, Potter. I'm glad that you risked everything for me."

"You risked even more to save me," I said, no longer able to feel angry that she had *pushed* me away now that she had explained her reasons. Cupping her face in my hands, I kissed her lightly on the lips. "So we're a team again?"

"I wouldn't ever want it any other way – whatever might happen," she said.

"Let's go and do what we do best," I said, taking her hand in mine.

"And what's that?" she asked.

"*Push* back," I smiled, rocketing up into the night sky with Kiera at my side.

Chapter Seven

Kiera

I wanted to tell Potter how I had agonised over the decision to save Sophie. I wanted to explain to him how it should have been us that was having a child together. As we had spoken outside the barn it had been on the tip of my tongue to tell him how Jack had come to me in my dreams and told me that Potter and I had a daughter. But I hadn't said anything. What would've been the point? I couldn't be sure that we had a daughter in the future or even if it was us that Jack was referring to – it could be another Kiera and Potter from another layer. I didn't even know if the dreams that I had about Jack were just that – dreams. Why muddy the water? Why tell Potter about a daughter that we might not ever share together? I didn't even know her name. Although Jack had told me about her he had never said what she was called. If I searched my dreams deep enough the most Jack had told me was that in his layer – mine and Potter's daughter was on trial for murder. So she couldn't be a child any longer – so if what Jack had told me was true he must be talking about something that had happened in my future – even a different layer – even if it happened at all.

All that really mattered to me now was that Potter was back. Someone had brought us back together – someone had seen a reason to do so. My instincts told me that it had been Lilly Blu. I was happy to follow Potter back to Hallowed Manor for now. He was right – perhaps we should find out the true reason as to why Murphy had killed Lilly Blu in this *where* and *when*. Despite the Murphy in this layer not being the guy I had come to see as some kind of surrogate father – he still didn't seem like the kind of man that would decapitate Lilly Blu and scatter her body over un-sacred ground. He must have had gone reason – if there could ever be a reason for doing such a thing. I couldn't believe he would do something like that just because she was a different species – a Lycanthrope. But if he was capable of murder, then that put Potter and I in real danger.

    Potter banked to the right and I followed, the tips of our wings almost touching. I glanced back as the night wind buffeted me. I looked up at those three fingered claws at the tip of each of my wings. I watched them open and close as if snatching hold of fistfuls of air and dragging me forward – faster and faster toward Hallowed Manor. Potter's black hair blew back from his face and his tatty wings rippled above him as he shot forward. England raced past beneath us – nothing more than a blurred patchwork of fields, hills, and valleys. We flew high above small villages and towns set amongst the hills. Very few lights twinkled back up at us from the dwellings below as those humans occupying them slept blissfully in their beds. Dawn was still a few hours off and I would need the cover of darkness if I were to go and investigate what the key Ravenwood had given me opened or led to. I couldn't risk running into Sophie, Hunt, or even Murphy. They would wonder why I was there at such an hour. And if I should come across Uri and Phebe I'd only have to undergo one of their interrogations. They would definitely ask where I'd been for the last few days. If I'd been late back to the Crescent Moon Inn by just a few minutes I'd been quizzed by them. Of course they tried to make their questions seem just like they were concerned for me and my wellbeing – but I knew there was more to it than that. What did it matter to them where I had been and why? But I knew it did, I just didn't know why.

Looking straight ahead, my long black and blue hair trailing like a mane behind me, I could see the hulking silhouette of Hallowed Manor in the distance. It sat behind the large stone wall that surrounded it on all sides. The water in the moat looked like black ice in the dark. I could see that the drawbridge was up as Potter and I swooped over the gatehouse. As I glanced down, I couldn't help but again be reminded that that was where we had shared our first kiss. I hadn't known it was Potter at the time – but he had never really believed that. Perhaps he was right – perhaps deep down I had really known that it was Potter I had been kissing in the gatehouse. But I'd continued to fight the urge to do so again until we had both found ourselves imprisoned in the caves hidden behind the Fountain of Souls. That's where we had first made love. Even back then I'd tried to tell myself that it had only happened because I feared that I was about to die – we both did – and it was just a desperate attempt to reach out for human contact before we were led to our deaths by the wolves. But I knew at that moment I was in love with Potter. If I hadn't been, then I would have never made love to him. He had been my first and last. Was that why I had been jealous about Sophie in the past? Was it because Potter had a past and I didn't? At some level, did I resent the fact that he had been intimate with another woman other than me? Of course I resented it. I had once resented Eloisa Madison – another woman that Potter had been intimate with. But she had been a wolf and Potter had killed her because of that, or so I had first believed, but he had later told me that the true reason he had killed her was because she had murdered several children. It was retribution for those crimes that he had so callously ripped out her heart. I glanced sideways at him as we swooped out of the sky and toward the summerhouse set in the woods of Hallowed Manor.

Together we dropped out of the night into the clearing set

amongst the trees. Side by side we both surveyed the treeline to make sure that we hadn't been seen. Peering through the darkness, I could see that we were alone. Without saying a word, Potter followed me across the clearing to the summerhouse. We climbed the wooden steps and took shelter in the shadows beneath the porch. Potter cupped his hands about his eyes and peered through the windows into the summerhouse.

Satisfied that we were alone, he turned to look at me and grinned. "Remember what we got up to on the floor in there, sweet-cheeks?"

"This place is full of memories," I said, glancing across the clearing and in the direction where Sophie had killed Ravenwood.

"Well you don't look very happy about that," Potter said, jarring me from my thoughts.

"Some of those memories are happier than others," I said.

"I just try to think about the happier ones," he said with a smile, pulling me close and planting a kiss on the tip of my nose.

"So what's your plan?" I asked him.

"To go and wake up that old-fart and..."

"You can't just march into the hospital wing in the middle of the night and start asking Murphy about why he cut Lilly Blu's head off," I said.

"I'll think of something," Potter shrugged, taking a cigarette and lighting it. He blew smoke up into the night air. "Everything will be just fine..."

"No fighting – no bloodletting," I warned him. "Speak to Murphy and get out. We can't risk anyone discovering you're not *their* Potter."

"I promise," he said, before kissing me once more on the tip of the nose.

I watched him head down the steps and across the porch, a stream of cigarette smoke trailing behind him. "See you later, alligator," I called out.

"In a while, crocodile," he said before stepping into the darkness and out of view.

Chapter Eight

Potter

From the treeline, I stood and looked across the vast lawns that stretched away to the front of Hallowed Manor. I watched it as I stood and finished my cigarette. Kiera had been right, the place did bring back plenty of memories and not all of them involved Kiera and me rolling around on the floor of the summerhouse having jiggy-jiggy. If I were to be honest some of the memories that now flooded my mind as I hid in the shadows and looked at the manor clawed at my heart. It was the place where I'd helped Murphy carry his dead daughters from and into the woods where we buried them. The sound of Murphy's gut-wrenching sobs suddenly filled my ears and haunted me. It hadn't been easy seeing my best friend consumed with grief. The best I'd been able to do was hug him. I hadn't known what to say – I'd never been very good with words. Were there even any words fitting for such an occasion? I couldn't think of one. But that had been the first time around. Had the second been any better? Not really. It was this place where Kiera had cracked up – literally. This is where the Elders had *pushed* us after our deaths in the Dust Palace deep within The Hollows. Me, Kiera, Kayla, and Isidor were all dead – we were all lost. That had been a fucking hard place to be. *How lucky would I be third time around?* I wondered, crushing the cigarette beneath my boot and setting off across the lawn. With my wings bristling behind me, I shot toward the manor, flying just inches above the finely cut grass. The moon was up and behind the manor casting long, drawn-out shadows out front. I kept to them as I crept around the front of the manor looking for any open window or door that I could use to gain access. Reaching the edge of the building, I snuck around the side of it. The door that led into the kitchen was set into the wall just ahead. I made my way toward it, legs bent at the knees and back stooped. I reached up and yanked on the door handle. It was locked tight. Looking back over my shoulder to make sure I couldn't be seen, or even worse wasn't being watched, I let my claws spring free from my fists. Closing them tight about the door handle, I yanked again and this time the lock came away in my hands.

"Shit," I muttered at the sound of the doorframe splintering and sounding like a lone firecracker exploding in the dead of night. With my heart suddenly pounding in my chest, I held my breath and listened. It was times like these I wished that I had Kayla with me. She could hear a fart coming from an arsehole a thousand yards away. She would know if my busting the lock had woken anyone inside the manor. But I didn't have Kayla with me. She was with the others in Snake Weed – in another layer.

When I was sure as I could be that I hadn't drawn attention to myself, I pulled open the door. It released a hideous wailing sound as it swung open on a set of rusty hinges. "Oh, for fuck's sake," I muttered under my breath before stepping once again into Hallowed Manor. I waited, crouched low by the legs of the long table that stretched the length of the kitchen and listened for any sound of movement. When I was sure that there was none, I stood up and crept forward, placing one foot as carefully as I could in front of the other. The door at the opposite end of the kitchen was ajar and I headed toward it. Pressing one eye to the gap, I peered out into the vast hall on the other side. It was very dark but there was no one that I could see. Content that I was alone and by some miracle hadn't disturbed anyone, I made my way across the hall and to the foot of the stairs. I climbed them as quickly as I could and up into the well of darkness above me. On the landing, I headed right and into the corridor that Kiera had once referred to as the forbidden wing.

Kiera had told me that Murphy had been injured and was resting in the hospital wing in the roof. I headed deeper into the dark that saturated the narrow passageway. At the end of it, I ran my fingers along the stone wall in search of the doorway that led to the spiralling staircase. Finding the door handle, I pushed on it and the door creaked open. Again, I paused mid-stride and waited. When no sounds came, I began to climb the staircase that wound its way around and around and up into the roof. The soles of my boots made scuffing noises against the stone steps. The narrow stairwell smelt of damp and dust. I reached the top and stood outside the door. I knew that my friend lay on the other side.

He's not your friend – not in this where and when, I heard Kiera whisper as if she had somehow managed to creep up on me in the dark. I glanced back but of course she wasn't there. No one was. Just me and my memories of Murphy. Slowly, I pushed against the door and it slowly swung open. I peered into the makeshift ward, and to be honest, it looked very much like I remembered it to be. There were four rows of beds down each side of the narrow attic. There were no windows and the only light came from a small gas lamp that was lit next to the nearest bed to me. On it lay Murphy. His head was tilted back, mouth open. If it wasn't for the thunderous roar of his snoring, he could have easily been mistaken for being a corpse. I glanced down and could see his scuffed out slippers placed neatly next to each other beneath the bed. His pipe and tobacco pouch sat on the table next to the gas lamp. The sheet was rolled down to his waist and I could see his bare chest. For such an old-fart, his chest and stomach was as sculpted as my own. It appeared that this

Murphy, despite being a grumpy old git at times, had made sure to keep himself fit.

I closed the door behind me then made my way toward the bed. I hadn't taken more than two steps, when Murphy's eyes snapped open and he looked straight at me.

"What are you creeping around in the dark for, Potter?" he suddenly barked.

Chapter Nine

Kiera

I waited for Potter to leave before turning to face the summerhouse. I needed to find out what the key Ravenwood had given me opened or led to. The only way of doing that was following the trail from where I'd last known Ravenwood to be. The night he had tried to poison Sophie, he raced away into the woods that surrounded Hallowed Manor. Had he been heading for the summerhouse? Was there something inside that the key opened? Closing my fist around the door handle, I pushed the door open. It smelt musty inside. I couldn't help but be reminded of the time I had spent here with Potter – with both Potters. This was where the Potter from this *where* and *when* had declared his love for me. It was the place where he had kissed me. But I had broken that kiss – pushed him away. I could hear myself telling him that he belonged to Sophie and that I wouldn't be that *other* woman in his life. I was so glad now that I had remained true to myself and not given in to the feelings that I'd had for the Potter from this layer. I had been right to believe that he wasn't my Potter and that he belonged to another. I was glad now that I had respected the relationship that he had with Sophie, regardless of what I thought of her. But as for Nev, I did have regrets about him. Not because we hadn't become anything more than friends, but because he had died and I hadn't been able to save him. I felt bad for Mavis too, that she had lost such a good friend. We both had. My regret was that we had become friends and just as I feared, he had died because of it. I should have kept my distance from him – but it was hard to do so. I'd had no one in this world and I'd needed a friend. Should I feel guilty about that? However short our friendship had been, I was glad that I'd met him. I was glad that my twenty-first birthday hadn't gone uncelebrated. I was happy that I'd had someone to share it with. Nev had made it a day that I would never forget and I would be eternally grateful to him for that. If I hadn't *pushed* Potter away, perhaps I could have spent my birthday with the man I truly loved. I only had myself to blame.

There was nothing in the summerhouse that I could see the key might open. There was no box, cupboard, or hatch. Just a bunch of old gardening tools and some mildew stained garden furniture. Closing the door behind me, I headed down the wooden steps that led from the porch and across the clearing. Although it was still night, the air was warm. I could hear the wind rushing through the leaves of the trees that surrounded the clearing. Reaching the treeline, I headed into the wood. Staring ahead, I made my way in the direction of the place where Sophie had killed Ravenwood. Why had she felt the need to kill him? I know he had tried to poison her, but I had saved her. She was safe. Was there another reason that Sophie had feared Doctor Ravenwood? Reaching the spot where Ravenwood had died, I peered down through the darkness as I brushed my fingertips over the spot where he had died. There was nothing to be seen. Had I left it too long to come back and investigate? Ravenwood had spoken of the willow trees, so standing up, I made my way toward them. They stood in a cluster like ancient men with curved spines, swaying their arms through the air just inches above the ground. Brushing the drooping branches aside and stooping forward as much as the branches, I stepped amongst the tired looking willow trees. It was the place where the half-breeds' graves had once been, but I doubted I would find such graves in the grounds of Hallowed

Manor, for as far as I knew there weren't any in this *where* and *when*. I pushed on through the overhanging branches until I suddenly stopped short. Had I been wrong in my assumption that there weren't half-breeds in this layer? If not, then why were there two gravestones sticking up out of the ground just ahead of me?

Slowly, I made my way toward them. When I was within touching distance of the headstones, I knelt before them. Unlike the headstones I had previously seen beneath the weeping willows, these weren't very old. Neither of them were cracked or masked green and yellow with moss. They had only been placed beneath the trees recently. There was an inscription written across both headstones that stood just feet apart. Screwing up my eyes and staring through the dark I read the names written across the graves and my heart broke.

Chapter Ten

Potter

"I couldn't sleep," I said. It was the best I could come up with.

"So you thought you'd skulk about up here?" Murphy said, eyeing me.

"I thought I'd come up and see how you were doing," I lied, edging nearer to the bed.

Murphy's hair stuck out at odd angles. He might have only just woken, but his eyes sparkled bright blue and were as keen and as sharp as ever. Despite my frequent quarrels with Murphy, I knew that he was no fool and I had to presume that *this* Murphy wasn't going to be any different. "So you thought you'd put your boots and overcoat on to come up here?"

"I've been out walking in the grounds – thought I'd clear my head a bit," I lied.

Propping himself up against his pillows, Murphy reached for his pipe and tobacco. He wedged a clump of it into the bowl of his pipe and lit it. "Well, sit down. Don't just stand there, you're making the place look untidy. Grab a seat," he said, the pipe drooping from the corner of his mouth.

There was a chair beside the bed. I could see that Murphy had hung his shirt neatly from the back of it. There were a pair of trousers too, and a long leather belt hung from the waist of them. Attached to the belt was a set of what looked like police-issue handcuffs. They reminded me of the cop uniforms we had both once worn. Were The Creeping Men like cops in this layer?

Knowing how precocious Murphy was about keeping his shirts and trousers looking pristine, I sat down on the chair, but was mindful to lean forward so as not to crease his clothing.

"I don't blame you for not being able to sleep, I keep one eye open most nights," he said.

"Why's that?" I asked, did he feel guilty about murdering Lilly Blu? Was that what kept him awake at night?

"Why do you think?" Murphy moaned. "Would you be able to sleep safely at night knowing that Mrs. Payne could pounce at any time, ready to give you a bed bath? She makes me feel vulnerable."

"Why don't you just tell her to fuck off?" I said. "That should do the trick."

"I've tried that but it seems that the harder I try and fight her off, the more persistent she becomes."

"Then why not just give her one and get it over with? You never know, with your track record with women you might put her off men for the rest of her life," I half grinned at him. I was trying to keep the whole thing causal – have some banter with him like I would've done with my friend.

He's not your friend – not in this where and when, I heard Kiera warn me again.

"Are you trying to be funny?" Murphy scowled at me.

My heart skipped a beat. How far could I push it with this Murphy? "I was just having a laugh with you that's all, you old fart. Where's your sense of humour?"

"Being molested by a senior citizen isn't funny, Potter," Murphy grunted before sucking on his pipe. "It's demeaning. She should know better at her age. Besides, I don't see why I should take any advice from you – your love life isn't exactly all boxes of chocolates and roses."

"What do you mean by that?" I took a cigarette from the

packet in my pocket and lit it.

Murphy half choked on a throat full of pipe smoke. "What do I mean? Have you forgotten that you turned Sophie and she's carrying your baby?"

"How could I forget," I said, trying to adopt the life of the Potter that Kiera had killed.

"So why are you trying to make matters worse for yourself by messing about with that girl, Kiera Hudson?" Murphy said, peering through a waft of pipe smoke at me.

"What do you mean messing about?" I said, trying to sound too startled.

"Oh, c'mon, give me a break, Potter," Murphy said. "I've seen the way you two look at each other. You're all over each other like a rash. It's embarrassing to watch. And I'll tell you something else for nothing – if Sophie finds out about what's going on with you and the girl Kiera, she'll have your balls. That Sophie is a jealous one."

What was he talking about? Kiera had said nothing had happened between her and the other me. She said they had just been friends. "What are you talking about? Nothing is going on between me and Kiera."

"Christ, you must really think I came down in the last shower," Murphy said. "Why did you go shooting off the other day?"

"What are you talking about?" I really now had no idea where this was going.

"You were here looking after Sophie after Ravenwood had tried to kill her, then you get a call from Kiera and you go rushing off and the next time I see you, you're creeping about up here in the middle of the night telling me you can't sleep because you've got lots on your mind. If I were you, I would leave the girl Kiera well alone. She seems like a nice kid and she doesn't need you messing with her head. Besides, I know for a fact that she's dead keen on that lad… what was his name? Nev, that was it."

"Nev? Who the fuck is Nev?" I spluttered. Was that the name of the guy that had once lived with Mavis Bateman? Had her lodger been called Nev? Hadn't he lived in the barn – in the barn where me and Kiera had just made love? Had Kiera and this Nev…? No, Kiera wouldn't do that to me. I felt my heart suddenly twist in my chest.

"I knew you was jealous of him," Murphy said, watching me through the cloud of smoke that bloomed from the end of his pipe.

"Jealous? What are you talking about?" I asked.

"Jeez, you should have seen your face when I told you that the boy, Nev, had taken Kiera to some fancy restaurant to celebrate her birthday…"

"Birthday?" I breathed. "It was Kiera's birthday?"

"Yeah, numb-nuts, and you went and wrecked it – just like you wreck everything you touch. Just couldn't bear the thought of her going on a date with that guy – I saw the jealousy in your eyes. Well, I'm telling you as a friend, keep away from Kiera Hudson. You've got a fiancée now and she's carrying your baby. And besides…"

"Besides what?" I shot at him, my heart feeling as if it had been wrung out to dry.

"I couldn't ever see a girl like Kiera being happy with someone like you."

"What's that s'posed to mean?"

"Just take a look at yourself, Potter," Murphy said. "You look like a sack of shit most of the time. And you can't string a coherent sentence together unless it's got the word fuck in it several times over."

"Bollocks," I scowled at him.

"See what I mean," Murphy laughed to himself. "You just can't help yourself. No, Potter, take it from me, a girl like Kiera needs a sensitive man in her life – someone with a bit of finesse – someone like that young artist, Nev."

"You don't know what you're talking about," I shot at him. "And how can you sit and tell me how to treat a woman when you ripped Lilly Blu's fucking head off."

"She deserved it," Murphy snapped, suddenly putting his pie down and sitting bolt upright on the bed.

"Oh yeah, why?"

Murphy looked at me agog. "Have you forgotten what she did?"

"Remind me," I hissed.

"She murdered the girl, Kayla, and the boy, Isidor," Murphy said.

Chapter Eleven

Potter

"What did you say?" I said, leaping out of my chair.

"How could you have forgotten so easily what she did to those kids?" Murphy said. "You were there with me, Potter, when we found her snout buried deep in the guts of our friends. Kayla and Isidor were one of us – or have you forgotten that, too? They were part of The Creeping Men."

Still reeling with shock at what Murphy had just told me, I tried to recover the situation and said, "No, I haven't forgotten. How could I?"

Murphy fixed me with a hard stare from where he still sat on the bed. But his face looked suddenly grim and distrustful of me. "You seem to have forgotten much, Potter – if that's who you really are."

"What's that s'posed to mean?" I said, trying not to break his stare – desperate not to show the slightest sign of weakness. "Who else could I be?"

"You could be a wolf," Murphy said, pulling back the sheet and swinging his legs over the side of the bed. He had a bandage wrapped about his stomach, but apart from that, he was naked.

"Get the fuck out of here," I half laughed. "Are you for real?"

"I've heard tales of wolves that can truly shapeshift – take on any form. So tell me, *Potter*, how did I get the limp?" Murphy asked, pulling himself up. He winced with pain, placing one hand to the bandage.

How did he get the limp in this *where* and *when*? The wolf, Inspector Harker, shot him once before – that's how he had come by the limp in the layer I had once come from.

"You were shot," I said, trying to sound as confident as I could.

"By whom?" he said squaring up to me.

I looked back at him.

"You shot me, Potter," he whispered.

I forced a smile. "I was just about to say that."

"Liar," Murphy roared.

"I'm sorry," I said.

"What for?" he said matching my stare.

"This," I said, driving my knee into his unprotected groin.

Murphy threw his hands to his lap and cupped himself there, bent forward at the waist. Seizing my chance, I pushed him back onto the bed. He groaned in agony but I knew it would only be a matter of moments before Murphy regained his strength. Pulling the belt from the trousers that had been hung over the back of the chair, I snatched free the set of handcuffs and hurriedly snapped them in place about his wrists and then to the bedstead.

"Unfasten me!" Murphy roared, yanking on the handcuffs as he wrestled to and fro on the bed. Fearing that his hollering might wake any others asleep in the manor, I tore a strip of the sheet free.

"I'm sorry, my friend," I said, before stuffing the strip of sheet into his mouth. "One day you might understand."

Murphy made a series of muffled choking sounds in the back of his throat.

"What's going on here?" I heard someone say.

I looked up to see a dishevelled-looking woman standing in the now open doorway to the hospital wing. Even though her grey hair stuck out like coiled springs from the sides of her head, and her face was lined with age, I recognised her at once. She wore a nightdress that looked as crumpled as her grim face.

"What's wrong with Jim?" Mrs. Payne said, glancing past me at Murphy who lay naked and secured to the bed. I couldn't help but notice how her eyes suddenly widened at the sight of him. Her eyes weren't filled with concern for him. It was sheer desire that I could see in them.

I looked back at the bed, then back at Mrs. Payne, who had already taken two more steps into the room and closer to Murphy handcuffed to the bed. "This is a little awkward and embarrassing, but it looks like Murphy's secret is out," I half smiled at her.

"Secret? What secret?" she said, unable to take her eyes off Murphy as he writhed on the bed, moaning and groaning behind the gag I had stuffed into his mouth.

"He's kinky…"

"I can see that," Mrs. Payne said edging ever nearer to the bed and Murphy. She wetted her wrinkled lips with the tip of her tongue.

"In fact, he asked me to tie him up tonight then go and find you…" I started, trying to fight the urge to grin from ear to ear.

"Oh, Jim, why didn't you just ask?" she said, stepping up to the bed and looking down at her prize.

"He's just a bit shy, I guess," I said, looking down at Murphy. He stared past Mrs. Payne at me, his eyes wide with fear. "And don't worry if he tries to resist or fight you off, it's all just part of the little games he likes to play."

"Should I go and get a bowl with some warm water and a sponge?" Mrs. Payne asked, sounding suddenly breathless.

"I think Jim is hoping for a little more than a bed bath

tonight, Mrs. Payne," I whispered while smiling down at Murphy.

He shook his head violently from side to side as if trying to work free the gag. I could only begin to imagine what abuse he might shower upon me if he were able.

"So I guess I better leave you two to your fun and games," I said, waving down at Murphy, the biggest grin I ever did have spread across my face. He tried to kick out at me with one leg, but I merely stepped away and headed for the door. Stepping out, I closed the door behind me.

As I headed down the stairs, I heard Mrs. Payne's breathless voice. "Don't look so scared, Jim. I'm not going to hurt you… or perhaps that's what you do want?"

Chuckling to myself, I headed back down the spiral staircase, Murphy's muffled cries ringing out in the darkness above me.

Chapter Twelve

Potter

Did I feel mean for leaving Murphy in the hands of Mrs. Payne? No – not really. Kiera had been right. The man in the attic wasn't my friend. He looked like him – sounded like him – but it wasn't the Murphy I knew. My friend wouldn't have been prepared to kill me for being a wolf. He might have killed me for leaving him chained to a bed for the likes of Mrs. Payne to have some fun with, but not for being a wolf. The Murphy I had just been speaking with would have killed me just like he had killed Lilly Blu. But hadn't he had good reason to do so? If what he said was true, Lilly had butchered and killed Kayla and Isidor in this *where* and *when*. Why had she done that? Whatever the reason, I had been right on insisting to Kiera that we come and find the true reason why Murphy had killed Lilly Blu. Could we now trust her? But more than that, could I trust Kiera? I hated myself for thinking such a thing, but if what Murphy had said was true, then Kiera hadn't been exactly honest with me. She had mentioned very little about the guy named Nev. They had obviously been close – close enough for him to invite Kiera out for her birthday. And when had that been? Shouldn't I have been there for that? Perhaps I could have been if Kiera hadn't *pushed* me away. It appeared that it hadn't taken Kiera long to start going on dates with another guy. How long had she been in this layer – this *where* and *when*? Had she been here much longer than it had taken for me to be led through the valley by Lilly Blu and into that shack? And what of this other Potter – this other me? Kiera had denied there had been anything between them out of respect for Sophie? After talking to Murphy, I now wasn't so sure that was entirely true.

Reaching the bottom of the stairwell, I made my way back through the darkness that saturated the corridor. I hadn't gone very far when I felt a hand grip my arm. Before I'd had the chance to pull away, I was being dragged into a dimly lit room. The only light came from two candles that shone from the table near to a window and a bed in the corner. I heard the door swing shut behind me and I spun around.

"Where have you been?" she asked, stepping into the light.

"Sophie?" I gasped.

"You sound surprised to see me," she said, coming forward and throwing her arms tight about me.

The nightie she wore was made of the flimsiest of material and I could feel her against me. I flinched away.

"What's wrong?" she asked, looking up into my face, her lips just inches from mine.

Oh, Christ, how was I going to get myself out of this one?

What's to get out of? the wolf suddenly asked, springing out of the darkness and to the forefront of my mind.

I screwed my eyes shut, willing the wolf to fuck off from where it had come from. In that moment that my eyes were closed, Sophie crushed her lips over mine.

Fuck me they feel so soft, the wolf howled deep inside of me. *They taste so sweet too.*

I pulled my face away from Sophie, breaking the seal she had formed over my lips.

"What's wrong?" she asked, looking a little startled – a little hurt by my rejection.

Yeah, what's wrong, Potter? She's fucking hot, man, the

wolf whispered in my ear. *Just look at her long blonde hair – blue eyes…*

She's not Kiera, I told the wolf.

And Nev wasn't you, but that didn't stop her…

"Shut the fuck up," I muttered out loud.

"What did you say?" Sophie asked.

"Nothing," I said, watching her brush slowly past me. She stopped in the centre of the room, just before the bed.

"Where have you been? I've been worried about you. Where did you rush off to that day?" Sophie asked me.

Was she talking about the day Murphy said I'd dropped everything to run off to be with Kiera? Had Murphy been correct about my other self and Kiera? Had there been something more between them than Kiera was letting on? And why wouldn't there have been – he looked like me – sounded like me. But Kiera would have said. Kiera wouldn't have lied to me – unless – unless she hadn't wanted to hurt my feelings. No, Kiera wouldn't have. The Potter from this layer was with Sophie. Kiera would have steered clear. She told me so – she told me that she didn't get involved with the other Potter because he was with Sophie, and she was pregnant.

And you believe that bullshit, do you? The wolf whispered inside of me. *Of course Kiera fucked the other Potter. Why wouldn't she? And she screwed the young artist dude too. You know it to be true. If she hadn't have screwed Nev's brains out, why didn't she talk more about him? Why not mention they had been out on a date together for her birthday? Kiera didn't tell you any of that because she had something to hide. She was hiding the fact that they had fucked.*

I screwed my eyes shut – anything to take away the image of Sophie standing in the candlelight by the bed before me. Anything to rid me of the wolf's voice. But no sooner had I closed my eyes, I saw Kiera lying naked on that bed in the barn. She was being made love to. She was crying out with joy. I inched closer to the bed, my heart aching, my intestines feeling like jelly. I had to know who it was that was causing her so much pleasure. I wanted it to be me. But as I reached the edge of the bed, the man who was moving over her looked up at me. It wasn't my face that I could see – not even that of the other Potter. That might have been a little more bearable. But the face I could see was that of a young man. He was handsome. He grinned at me, then went back to pleasuring Kiera. I looked down at her face and could see the joy splashed across her face.

I couldn't bear to watch. I felt the urge to vomit. I snapped open my eyes. Sophie had moved closer to me.

"Potter, what's wrong?" she asked, reaching for my hand with one of her own.

"I've got to get out of here," I mumbled, stumbling blindly for the door.

"But you've only just got back," Sophie said, taking me in her arms. She pressed the side of her face against my chest. I could smell the shampoo she had used in her long, thick blonde hair. It made me feel suddenly heady. The side of her face and hair felt so soft against my hard chest.

She smells good, doesn't she? the wolf whispered. *She feels good too. But you already know that, don't you, Potter? You've made love to her before. You know how damn good that felt. You've never truly forgotten. You know it – we both know it.*

Opening my eyes, I eased Sophie from my arms.

She looked at me. "You seem upset about something, what's wrong?"

"Nothing's wrong," I said, turning for the door again.

"Come to bed, Sean," I heard her whisper. "I can make you feel better. We can make each other feel better."

Reaching the closed door, I glanced back. Sophie now stood naked at the foot of the bed, the nightie pooled about her feet. Her hair cascaded over her shoulders, barley covering her breasts. Her round hips looked so smooth in the dim candlelight. Her thighs...

I snapped my eyes closed again.

Take her, Potter, the wolf tempted me. *Go on, you know you want to. Who wouldn't want to? Just open your eyes and take another look at her. She's fucking gorgeous. And look at those titties. They're so firm and pert they could poke your eyes out.*

But I love Kiera, I told the wolf.

But does she love you? the wolf asked. *She had her fun with the other you and the artist dude. You know she did. And so what if you fuck Sophie, who is ever going to know? It's only you and Sophie here.*

Sophie might tell Kiera... I started to reason.

So screw Sophie then... kill the bitch, the wolf suggested. *She won't be able to tell Kiera then.*

"Don't you find me beautiful?" I heard Sophie suddenly ask.

I opened my eyes again to find that she had once again crossed the room toward me. She was so close that I could smell the perfume of her naked flesh. With a shake of her bare shoulders, a set of glistening black wings sprung from her back. They hummed gently on either side of her.

"Don't you like what you turned me into?" As she spoke, I could now see the tips of her fangs jutting from each corner of her mouth behind her full pearly lips. The wolf was right, she did look incredibly beautiful.

The wolf roared inside of me. *Take her!*

And as it did, Sophie took one of my hands in hers, and brought it up to her breasts. My heart raced as I could feel the heat of her flesh just within reach.

"No," I said. "I can't do this. I'm no longer who you think I am."

Yanking my hand free of her hold, I turned around and yanked open the bedroom door.

Sophie grabbed hold of me and spun me around with such force that I struck the side of the doorframe. Every bone in my body seemed to rattle. I was surprised by her strength. "It's because of her, isn't it?" Sophie hissed into my face, her fangs glistening in the candlelight.

"What the fuck are you talking about?" I said, pushing her away from me.

"You're in love with *her* – with Kiera Hudson!" she shrieked, bright eyes suddenly bulging. I couldn't help but wonder what kind of monster the other Potter had created here.

"You don't know what you're talking about," I said, taking another step closer to the open doorway. I wasn't now keeping up the pretence of being the other Potter to protect myself, but to protect Kiera. If Sophie believed that I had become Kiera's lover, it might put her in danger.

"I can smell her on you," Sophie said, springing forward and sniffing the air about me. "You've been with her. How could you? I'm carrying your child. We are to be married."

"You don't know what you're talking about..."

"Don't lie to me!" Sophie screamed, raking the air in front of my face with her hands that now looked more like claws.

"I let you turn me – I became a monster for you – and this is how you repay me. This is how you repay our unborn child," she said, placing one claw flat against her stomach. "How could you do this to me and our daughter, Abbie?"

"What did you say her name was going to be?" I asked, feeling as if I'd been suddenly slapped in the face.

"Abbie," Sophie spat. "Don't tell me you've forgotten our child's name already?"

I had heard that name before after Noah had pushed me through the layers to go in search of the photographer. In that layer I had been haunted by a little girl. On retuning back to my own layer, I told Lilly Blu about that little girl. Lilly had said that the girl's name had been Abbie. She said that the girl was my daughter from another layer – a layer where I was married to Sophie. How had Lilly known such a thing?

"You chose that name," Sophie said, looking at me, tears standing in her eyes. "Don't I – doesn't our baby mean anything to you anymore?"

"I'm sorry, I can't do this," I said, turning and heading back out into the corridor. As I headed into the darkness, I heard Sophie scream. Reaching the top of the staircase, I raced down into the hall. I looked back over my shoulder and could see Sophie standing at the top of the stairs. She had pulled on some jeans and a hoodie. From beneath the hoodie I could see a murderous look in her eyes.

"If I can't have you, Potter, than no one will," I heard her hiss from the top of the stairs. I pulled on the door handle of the main door, but it was shut tight. Diving into the shadows, I made my way along the edge of the hallway. From the dark, I watched Sophie slowly descend the stairs. She opened and closed her claws as if grabbing fistfuls of darkness. I inched my way toward a door set into the wall. I could see that it was slightly ajar. Just as Sophie reached the bottom stair, I reached the door and silently snuck inside. From the room I now found myself in, I peered through the gap out into the hall.

"Come out, Potter," Sophie sneered as I watched her scan the dark. "What have you got to be scared of? What, are you scared of me? Scared I might tell on you? Give up your secrets?"

What was she talking about? What secrets did the other Potter have?

She came close to the door from which I hid behind. I held my breath. It wasn't that I was scared of Sophie, I could snap her neck as easily as a piece of kindling, but I'd promised Kiera there would be no bloodshed. And besides, there was no way I was going to fight a pregnant woman. I pressed myself flat behind the door as I heard Sophie approach the room. As I readied myself for her to step inside and discover me, I heard her stop short just outside. I waited, I listened. Was she playing games with me? Then to my relief, I heard her move away in the opposite direction of my hiding place. Placing my eye to the gap in the door once more, I watched Sophie head back across the hall to the main doorway. She reached up and threw the bolt. Had she heard a noise outside? She pulled open the door and stepped outside into the grounds of Hallowed Manor. Bent double, I crossed the room that I now found myself in. Each wall was lined with bookcases. There was a desk and a threadbare looking rug on the floor. Behind the desk was a window that was covered with thick drapes. I teased them apart and looked outside. A thin strip of moonlight fell over my shoulder and partially lit the room. Sophie passed by on the other side of the window and I flinched backwards.

"Potter, come out, come out wherever you are," I could hear her calling.

I waited for the sounds of her voice to grow muffled, then stepped away from the window. I knew that I had to get back into the woods and to Kiera without being discovered by Sophie. I couldn't afford to let her discover us together. Setting off across the room, I suddenly stopped halfway. I had seen something from the corner of my eye that had grabbed my attention. I turned to face one of the many bookshelves that lined the study walls. The moonlight that streamed through the open curtains fell across one of the bookcases and it was one of the books on it that had grabbed my attention. I headed for the book and took it from the shelf. *Wind in the Willows*, the title read. Hadn't Ravenwood once before left a book for Kiera to find with the very same title? Hadn't we found it in his house on the outskirts of Wasp Water? Hadn't Ravenwood recently told Kiera that he could hear the wind in the willows before giving her that key and dying? I thumbed through the pages, but couldn't see anything of real interest. I then shook the book to see if anything fell from it. When nothing did, I went to place it back onto the bookshelf, when I saw what looked like a safe fitted into the wall behind where the book had concealed it only moments ago. There was a small keyhole, but I didn't have the key. Was the key that Kiera had in her coat pocket – the one that fitted the lock to the safe? If it was, I couldn't risk bringing Kiera back to the manor with Sophie stalking the grounds wanting our blood.

    Reaching into the gap where the book had once sat, I released my claws, and yanked free the lock. It came away in a puff of brick dust. Once it had settled, I peered into the hole that I had made. There was a beige coloured envelope. Reaching inside, I took hold of it and pulled it out. Stepping into the moonlight, I opened the envelope and peered at what lay inside.

Chapter Thirteen

Kiera

I stumbled backwards and away from Kayla's and Isidor's graves. Is this where they had gone? When I'd asked Murphy, and even their own father, Lord Hunt, what had happened to Kayla and Isidor, they had both simply told me that they had gone away. They hadn't gone anywhere other than to their graves. And as I stood and peered at their headstones through the swaying branches of the willow trees, there was a part of me that wasn't too surprised by the fact that they were dead already in this layer. It was slowly dawning on me that in each of the layers I had been *pushed* into, both Kayla and Isidor had met their deaths at a very young age and usually at the same time or within a very short period from each other. They had both been murdered by Luke Bishop as we had travelled across The Hollows in search of the Dust Palace. After my own death at the hands of my brother, Jack, I had woken to find myself and my friends *pushed* into another layer. There, both Kayla and Isidor had been murdered. Each of them killed by their father on the side of a mountain – their bodies buried in the snow. How had my friends met their deaths in this *where* and *when*? And just as I now stood and looked down at their graves, I knew I had done so once before in the layer I'd recently been *pushed* from. *How many layers were there?* I wondered as I made my way slowly away from the two graves and back toward the summerhouse where I had arranged to meet Potter. How many Kaylas, Isidors, Murphys, and Potters were out there? How many *of me* existed in the different *wheres* and *whens* that there seemed to be? And which one was real — which one of us was the true Kiera Hudson? Which one of us had been the first? Wasn't I the true one? Wasn't Potter the real Potter? But the Potter from this *where* and *when* had believed that he was real too. Just like the Murphy from this *where* and *when* believes he is the real deal as Potter would say. But was he? Were any of us? What made our lives any more real than the others? All I could *see* was that there were similarities between the differing versions of me and my friends. We all worked in law enforcement in some way or another in the different layers. We all gravitated to the same locations, like Hallowed Manor, the Ragged Cove, the Fountain of Souls, Wasp Water, Snake Weed, and many others. It would seem that each of us was a faint reflection of the other — but living in different layers — *wheres* and *whens*. Murphy had described the layers once as sheets of tracing paper that were laid over each other. Sometimes those sheets of tracing paper got shifted — pushed — out of place and you could see the other sheets beneath. Jack had told me that people were *pushed* through the layers when they died. He believed that there was no such thing as death — that when we died we were simply *pushed* into another layer. Is that how Jack justified his killing? Did he believe that he was simply *pushing* his victims instead of killing them? But Noah had described it as something else altogether. As we had sat alone in that Grand Railway station, he had described the layers and the *wheres* and *whens* as a vast series of railway tracks — a network of points and junctions with signal boxes set along each route. He said it was when those levers in those derelict signal boxes got *pushed* and *pulled* was when we got diverted onto a different path — a different set of tracks — into a different *where* and *when*. So was my life and that of my friends a journey along those tracks — was everyone's lives like that? Did it work the same for humans or just for supernatural beings? Was that what immortality truly was for beings like me? Did we not so much travel the length of time but through it? Through the different layers – being reborn into our old selves – going around and around on those tracks that Noah had described. And if so – could we never get off? Could we never get the train to stop when we'd had enough? Wouldn't we eventually envy the humans who could die and truly move on to something better? Was immortality, in fact, nothing but a curse? A never-ending journey of pain and heartache that we could never truly escape because there was no such thing as death for us? A life without end…

"I thought I might find you skulking out here," someone said. "I didn't think you would be too far away from Sean."

Jarred from my thoughts, I looked up in the direction of the voice. Sophie was coming down the steps of the summerhouse and toward me at speed.

"Everything was going just fine until you showed up!" she screeched, pulling back the hood of the sweater she wore. Her eyes blazed like two black stones and her lips were rolled back to reveal her fangs. With wings suddenly tearing from her back, she launched herself at me.

In an instance the wolf was right at the forefront of my mind – leaping out of the darkness to protect me.

"Back off!" I hollered, not at Sophie but at the wolf inside of me. The wolf didn't scare me – I was more scared of what it was capable of. It had torn Potter's throat out when fearing that I was under attack from him. The wolf snarled deep inside of me as if yanking on a taut leash that I couldn't see. It reared up on its hind legs as if untameable. It barked over and over, causing my head to throb and body to shake. *"Back!"* I hissed.

"No! You back off, Hudson!" Sophie roared, cutting the air in front of my face with her claws.

I darted away. She looked startled by the speed in which I

had moved. I was now on the other side of the clearing and well out of her reach. She spun around to face me.

"Sophie, you've got to listen to me – you don't understand," I said, trying to keep my voice calm and the wolf at bay. I couldn't hurt Sophie – I *wouldn't* hurt Sophie – she was carrying a child inside of her. Wasn't it bad enough that I had killed the man who had put it there?

"Oh, I understand all right," Sophie said, heading back across the clearing toward me again. Her claws hung at her sides and her hair billowed about her shoulders. "You've been sleeping with Sean – you've been trying to steal him away from me. You've been trying to steal my baby's father." She placed one of her claws to her stomach as if protecting her unborn child.

"No, that's not true," I insisted, taking a step backwards as she grew ever nearer.

"You've come to kill me – just like Ravenwood tried to kill me," Sophie said. "You just couldn't bear a human becoming like you. Being in love with one of you."

"That's not true," I repeated, trying to stay calm as the wolf reared up again inside me, her jaws gnashing open and closed.

"It is true!" Sophie screeched, making fists with her claws. She was so close now, I could see tears of rage streaming down her cheeks and off her chin.

"Why then did I save you?" I asked, willing the Vampyrus forward inside of me. If I was going to have to defend myself, I'd rather do so with her than with the wolf.

"To drag out my suffering and torment," Sophie said. "You wanted me to be alive to watch you steal Sean away from me. Well, I'm not going to let you take him. He's mine." Sophie shot forward, claws out. I darted to the right. Her claws sliced through nothing but the space where I'd been standing a fraction of a second ago. She spun around to face me again, head down, fangs drooling. Screaming, she shot forward at me again. This time faster – her anger and fury giving her greater speed. One set of claws sliced through my upper arm. Her claws felt like razorblades that had been coated with molten lava as they ripped apart the upper sleeve of my coat and the flesh beneath it. I cried out, glancing down at the ragged tears that now zigzagged the length of my arm. But it wasn't blood or even raw flesh that I could see seeping from the cuts she had made. All I could see was silky black fur.

Sophie saw it too. "What the fuck? You're a wolf!"

"Please, Sophie," I begged her as the wolf now broke free of that thin piece of rope I had it tethered to deep inside of me. "I don't want to hurt you."

"Filthy wolf!" Sophie cried out, swiping once more at me with her claws. She hit me so hard in the side of the head, that I was lifted off my feet and thrown back across the clearing.

As I spun through the air, the world turned red. The sky, the leaves on the trees, and the moon – all them now a crimson as if drenched in blood. At first I wondered if Sophie had split my head open and blood was now gushing from a hideous wound and into my eyes. But I couldn't feel the warm and sticky sensation of blood flowing from any part of me. All I could feel was the shape of my ears, eyes, nose, and mouth changing as it took on the form of the wolf. Colliding with a tree and sending up a spray of dead leaves and broken branches, I howled in pain. I slumped to the ground. I didn't land on all fours but on both feet. I looked down at myself and could see that I hadn't fully turned into the wolf. I was in that place somewhere between wolf and human – where my eyes, nose, and mouth were more cat-like in appearance than wolf. My hair was thicker and sat about my shoulders in thick glistening blue lengths. I looked down at my claws and they were black and sharp. I felt something swish behind me, and I glanced back over my shoulder not to see my wings, but a tail swishing back and forth in the night breeze.

"How could Sean have had sex with you – wolf?" Sophie screamed, racing across the clearing at me. Her long blonde hair looked almost white as it streaked out behind her in the moonlight. Her black wings shone as if showered with glitter. She launched herself at me.

But this time I didn't dart away, I drove her backwards with the heels of my hands. I yanked hard on the wolf inside me, not letting it come forward any more – unwilling to let it fully consume me and turn me into a full wolf. Sophie shot back through the air. Her wings rippled behind her, breaking her fall and keeping her just feet above the ground.

"Fight me," she hissed, sensing that I wouldn't.

"No, Sophie," I said, lowering my claws and taking a deep breath. "I won't hurt you – you have a baby inside..."

Before I'd had the chance to finish, Sophie was skimming across the clearing again toward me – her body no more than an inch above the ground. When she was nearly upon me, she swooped up through the air, raking at my flesh again with her claws. I cried out as she opened another ragged set of lines across my midriff. This time I did see blood seeping from me. I covered the cuts with one claw and raised the other as Sophie darted forward to launch other attack. She batted my claw away with one of her own. Her other claw lunged toward my face. I jerked my head back, but not soon enough. I felt her seething claws rake down the side of my neck as I twisted my head away. I felt the hot, sticky gush of blood. The wolf howled inside of me, leaping up and fighting to be truly set free. But I wouldn't release it. I couldn't. For I knew that if I did, I would kill Sophie. I would rip her throat out and gorge myself on her heart. And so I would not only have killed her but the life she carried inside of her.

"Please listen to me," I cried out, blood now gushing into my mouth.

Sophie shot forward again, driving her nails into my shoulder. I cried out, dropping to my knees.

"I thought you would've had more fight in you, Hudson," Sophie roared, driving the heel of her boot into my upturned face.

I heard the sound of bones breaking. Was it my nose? My cheekbone? I couldn't be sure, but it felt as if my skull was being caved in as Sophie drove her boot down again into my face. Blood gushed from my mouth and nose. It felt hot and thick like treacle.

I covered my face with my claws. I peered up through them and everything looked so red. Sophie looked red as she repeatedly kicked and stabbed at me with her claws.

"I thought you would have enjoyed a good fight!" Sophie screamed. "Or is the only thing that you're truly good at is stealing other women's men?"

"I saved you," I murmured over a throat full of blood. The wolf barked and howled inside of me as it worked its way up into a rapid frenzy. "Hush," I said trying to calm it.

"No, I won't hush!" Sophie screamed at me, before driving her boot over and over into my side. I heard the sound of more bones breaking. "I want Sean to know what a cheating, filthy little whore you really are. I want Sean to know you died a coward, curled up on the floor like a lame dog, too scared to even fight me. I'm gonna drag your fucking corpse back to the manor and show him what a filthy, cheating dog you really are..."

"I know what she is and I love her with all my heart," I heard someone say.

I peered up through my bloodstained claws to see Potter loom up out of the darkness behind Sophie. Before Sophie even had a chance to turn and see who it was that had spoken, her heart was exploding out of her chest with Potter's claws fixed firmly about it.

"No," I murmured, as I watched Sophie drop to her knees, then slump forward hitting the ground next to me. With her head just inches from mine, I looked into her dead black eyes as they stared back into mine. "I'm sorry I couldn't save you," I whispered, before darkness took me.

Chapter Fourteen

Kiera

"Hey, sis," I heard a voice whisper. "Kiera, wake up. It's me, Jack."

My long lashes fluttered as I struggled to open my eyes. "Jack?" I whispered, not knowing where I was. My head and body ached. I felt like I had been run over by a steamroller. I could feel something hot against my face. I tried to open my eyes again but the light on the other side of my lids was so bright that I closed them again.

"Am I dead?" I croaked, my throat feeling dry and sore.

"I fucking hope not because that would mean I'm dead too," I heard Jack say. "But then again perhaps we are both dead. Anyway, who gives a crap? I'm just glad to see you again even, if you do look like a sack of shit."

"Like shit?" I mumbled. I struggled to open my eyes again.

"You look beat-up real bad," Jack said from the other side of my lids. "Who did you get into a fight with this time? King-fucking-Kong by the looks of it."

"Sophie Harrison," I said, fragmented images of her attacking me swimming in the darkness behind my closed eyes.

"I hope you killed the bitch," he said.

"No, Potter did," I whispered, my lips feeling swollen and cracked.

"Finally grown some balls then, has he?"

"Why do you hate him so much?" I said, trying to open my eyes again.

"What's to like about him?" Jack said.

As my eyes slowly opened, I saw a dark shape in the light. It swam back and forth like an oil slick in a vat of milk. Slowly it took on a shape – the outline of a man. Jack. As he came into focus, I could see that his face was close to mine, as if he were inspecting me. I looked over his shoulder and could see the sun shining like a flat silver disc in the sky behind him. With his face so close to mine as he inspected the cuts and bruises, I could see that he looked younger – a lot younger. His skin was no longer a patchwork maze of age-defying wrinkles and grooves. His flesh no longer looked paper thin like it had been pulled too tight over his skull. Jack's eyes were no longer sunk into his face like two dark pits. My brother now looked as if he was in his early thirties – perhaps even late twenties. His skin was smooth as stone and there was a spattering of light coloured whiskers over his chin and sides of his face. His eyes were as gold in colour as the sun I could see over his shoulder. And the hair that hung from his baseball cap was blond, thick, and long and onto his shoulders. I struggled to comprehend the utter transformation that appeared to have taken place since I'd last seen him.

"You look... you look..."

"Different," he said, looping his arms through mine and propping me up. I looked about myself and could see that I had been lying on a wooden bench outside an ancient railway station in a desert that stretched away for miles in each direction. It was then I heard the familiar sound of unoiled hinges wailing in the arid breeze that blew up puffs of sand about our feet and across the station boardwalk. I looked up at the sign that swung slowly back and forth above our heads. Written across it were the words, 'Welcome to The Great Wasteland Railway'.

The last time I had seen that sign and the remote railway station was in the picture that Mavis Bateman had given to

Potter. Standing outside the station with the sign in the background had been Potter's mother, Joan, and her partner, Amity. They had looked happy, their smiles smeared with chocolate.

Were they here now? Could I find Potter's mother for him? I tried to get up off the bench. I cried out as a knot of pain unravelled within me.

"Take it easy, sis," Jack said, tucking one arm about my shoulders and helping me to my feet. I shuffled forward with him at my side. It was then I noticed that he wasn't as tall or as thin as he had once been – stretched out of shape by the hate and anger that burned within him. Jack couldn't have been any taller than six-foot now, and was of stocky to medium build.

"You look good," I said, trying to force a smile through my pain at him.

"I know," he smiled back.

And that was something else I noticed. His smile no longer looked like it belonged on the face of some crazy – some frenzied killer. It was warm and dare I say it – a friendly and welcoming smile. I searched his eyes for any spark of the wolf that had once stared back at me from behind them. But his eyes, like mine, were a bright hazel. I could see no sign of the serial killer I had once known.

"What happened to you?" I breathed, trying to get a grip on the pain that haunted every part of my body. Sophie really had given me a good beating it seemed.

"Enough talk for now, let me get you inside and out of the sun," Jack said, steering me along the dust covered boardwalk and into the small station come ticket office. Before stepping through the doorway, I glanced back at the set of rust coated railway tracks that snaked away in either direction across the desert.

"Take a seat," Jack said guiding me slowly across the

waiting room that also doubled as some type of café. There were several tables with chairs scattered at regular intervals, people sat at them and I scanned the faces in search of Joan and Amity. I couldn't see them. One or two of them glanced at Jack and me as he steered me to a table by a grime-smeared window. The window pane was cracked in one corner and covered in sand that had been carried across the desert. It was hot in the station café. A fan turned lazily overhead but it did nothing to ease the almost suffocating heat. I loosened the neck of my hoodie that I wore under my coat. It was then that I realised for the first time since waking that I no longer looked half wolf – half human, but was dressed again in my clothes. I stared at my pale reflection in the window as Jack set off across the café to a counter where an old woman wearing a mucky looking tabard was serving tea from a giant pot. I peered at the dark swelling around my eyes, and how my bottom lip was puffed out like I'd been given a shot of Collagen that had gone hideously wrong. There was dried blood around my nose and on my chin. I wiped it away with a napkin that had been placed on the table.

"Get that down you," Jack said, setting down a cup of tea before me. "It will have you feeling better in no time."

After sliding my coat off and placing it on the seat beside me, I picked up the cup of tea with both hands and took a sip. I grimaced.

"Too hot?" Jack asked.

"Too sweet," I said.

"It will do you good – get your strength up."

As I took another sip, I looked past him and over at the empty ticket booth where I guessed tickets were punched out and sold. Next to the booth were a row of levers. Above them were the words PUSH and PULL. Next to the levers stood a jukebox. Like the window next to me, a crack ran down the front of it. I looked away at some of the people sitting at the tables in the railway café.

"Do you know any of these people?" I asked Jack.

"Not really," he shrugged, glancing about the room. "I've spoken to one or two of them in the past when I've come here in search of you." He then pointed to a man who sat alone in the opposite corner who stared blankly out of the window. He had thick dark curly hair. He was smoking as he looked out across the desert on the other side of the window – like he was waiting for someone. "He's one of us – a wolf – but from another where and when. Got himself pushed. He looks nice enough. Apparently he was the last of the Lycanthrope from the layer he got pushed from. It was his girlfriend that pushed him in the end. I'm not sure why – I couldn't give a shit really, nothing to do with me. He just sits and stares out of the window."

"Why?" I asked, peering at the man over the rim of my teacup.

"I think he's waiting for her – you know – hoping that she will get pushed one day too."

"What's his name?" I asked.

"I'm not sure – something weird," Jack said taking off his baseball cap and arming sweat from his brow. "Thad or something like that."

"What about him?" I said, nodding in the direction of a guy who was sitting just a few tables away from us. He wore a smart black suit and tie with waistcoat. A tall black hat was on the table next to him and his whole attire looked like he was from the Victorian era. His black hair was immaculately cut and his pale face was clean shaven.

Jack glanced in the direction that I was looking. "Cop," Jack said. "Some police officer from 1800's London. I don't know too much about him. I've heard him being referred to by some of the others that pass through here as Inspector Creature. But that's about as much as I know."

"Have you ever seen two women here?" I asked. "One was called Joan – the other Amity."

"Not that I remember." Jack shrugged. "Why do you ask?"

"It's not important," I said, taking another sip of the tea.

"You wouldn't have asked, if it wasn't important," he said.

I looked across the table at him. "What are we doing here, Jack? What are these other people doing here?"

"The dead like traveling the railways, I guess," he said.

"Are we dead? Did Sophie kill me?"

"You're not dead, Kiera. You're probably lying unconscious someplace... getting over the kicking that you've just had."

"And what about you?"

"I'm asleep in my bed in someplace far, far away from here – if this really is a here – a where or a when. We're dreaming about each other again. When we do then we meet for some reason. I don't know why? I try not to think about it. I just try and enjoy it – enjoy seeing my kid sister again."

"So this place is like a waiting room of sorts?" I asked him.

"Perhaps," he shrugged. Then with a smile, he added, "Look, I don't really give a fuck – I'm just glad that we're here right now. Why do you have to always be trying to figure stuff out? See stuff? Just kick back and relax."

We both sipped our tea. I glanced back out of the window and caught my reflection again. Those bruises about my eyes and jawline were no longer black and purple but a patchy green, yellow, and mauve. My lower lip seemed to be a little less swollen. My stomach, ribs, and back didn't seem so stiff with pain. I sipped more of the sweet tea.

"What is this stuff?" I asked.

"Tea," he said right back.

"It's good."

"I told you it would be," he smiled again.

"So what happened... I mean, what happened to you?" I said.

He put down his cup. "Your daughter happened to me – that's what happened. She's been helping me – helping me to fight the wolf – tame the fucker inside of me."

I stared back across the table at my brother. "Look, Jack, are you sure that she's my daughter? Potter and I don't have a daughter."

"Not yet, maybe, but one day," Jack said.

"But that's what I don't understand," I told him. "When do Potter and I have a daughter? Does it happen in our future – in another layer?"

Jack shrugged his shoulders at me again. He seemed a lot less intimidating. There would have been a time when I would have feared questioning him. He appeared more relaxed now – easier going and less confrontational. "All I know is that she's your daughter."

"How can you be so sure? And how do you know that this girl isn't the daughter of a completely different me and Potter from some other where and when?"

"Because she talks about you two all of the time – she misses the both of you," Jack said.

"Misses us?"

"You both died," Jack said. "But statues were made of you – look I've told you all this before."

"I just find it hard to believe..."

"Perhaps you just don't want to believe..."

I frowned back at him. "What does that mean?"

"All I'm saying is that I know you and Potter have a daughter..."

"What's her name?" I shot at him.

"Cara," Jack said, a smile forming at the corners of his lips. His whole face seemed to light up as he pictured her in his mind's eye. "Cara Hudson."

"Wouldn't her last name be Potter if she truly is our daughter?"

"Perhaps you and Potter never get hitched – perhaps you spend what time you have left together bitching and fighting like you always do," Jack said.

"I don't know, Jack… I'm not so sure that this Cara…."

"Potter is going to give you a ring," Jack suddenly cut in. "The ring once belonged to his mother."

"How do you know about that ring?" I asked.

"You told Cara that story. You told her that the ring you will one day wear was given to you by Potter and that it had once belonged to his mother. How would I know that, Kiera – how would Cara know that if you hadn't have told her when she was growing up?"

I stared back across the table at Jack. Over his shoulder I thought I saw someone standing in front of the jukebox. He was dropping coins into the slot. The man had his back to me, but I could see what looked like black flames licking the side of his neck. With my mouth falling open, I pushed my chair back from the table where I sat with Jack and stood up. Now that I was standing, I could see that the young man was holding a crossbow in his free hand. Music started to seep from the speakers fitted into the front of the ancient looking jukebox. Although faint, I recognised the song. It was Heroes by David Bowie.

"Isidor?" I murmured, my heart suddenly skipping a beat with delight.

The young guy who stood before the jukebox looked back over his shoulder and smiled at me. It was Isidor!

"Isidor," I said, stumbling around the edge of the table. I

just wanted to run to him. To fold him in my arms and hold him tight and never let go. My thigh thumped into the table and I stumbled forward. The music began to swell. It grew louder and louder until it was almost deafening.

I looked up at where Isidor still stood by the jukebox. As if my legs had suddenly become entangled with each other, I fell forward. "Isidor!" I called out, my words drowning beneath the song now booming from the jukebox.

He came forward, reaching down for me with his free hand.

"Let me help you up," he smiled down at me. His eyebrow piercing glinted in the sunlight that fought to stream into the café through the dust-covered windows.

I closed my fingers around his. His flesh felt cold. He pulled me to my feet and held me in his arms.

"Isidor," I gasped, holding him tight, so glad to see my precious friend again.

"You're dreaming, Kiera," he whispered in my ear.

"Dreaming?" I said back.

"Isidor is dead. Murphy told me that bitch Lilly Blu killed him and...

Chapter Fifteen

Kiera

"...she killed Kayla," Potter said, holding me close to him.

I eased myself back in his arms and looked into his face. It was speckled with blood. "Potter?"

He smiled back at me. "The one and only."

I felt dazed and confused. "Where's Isidor? Where's Jack gone?"

"You must have been dreaming or hallucinating," Potter said concerned. "You took a pretty good beating from Sophie..."

"Sophie," I gasped, pulling away and looking all about me. We were no longer in the grounds of Hallowed Manor. I was standing in what appeared to be some small cave or hollow.

I shook my head. "Where am I?"

"In the valley – not too far from that shack where Lilly Blu *pushed* me," Potter explained.

"How did we get here?" I mumbled, stepping away from him and heading slowly toward the mouth of the cave. I looked out. The sun was fading overhead as the night slowly encroached upon it, sucking out its warm rays and casting it into shadow. I could see that I was standing in one of the caves that had been hollowed into the side of the valley. The valley lay below like a giant fissure in the earth. It stretched away in either direction for as far as I could see. There was no sound across the valley. It was as if while I'd been unconscious there had been some great war, wiping out every living thing other than Potter and me.

"How did I get here?" I asked, turning to face Potter. I

noticed a small fire burning at the rear of the cave. What looked like two skinned rabbits had been placed on makeshift skewers above the flames.

"I brought you here," Potter said. "Sophie nearly killed you..."

"Sophie," I said, screwing my eyes shut. In the darkness I saw Potter looming out of the shadows and driving his fist into her chest and ripping out her heart.

"She's dead," Potter said.

I snapped open my eyes. "She was pregnant."

Potter raised an eyebrow in my direction. "Was she?"

"What do you mean?"

Potter took me gently by the arm and led me across the cave toward the fire. "Sit," he said. "You need to rest. Your wounds look like they've healed pretty quickly – perhaps there is an upside to being a wolf after all."

As I sloped down against the cave wall, I put one hand to my lips. They no longer felt swollen or out of shape. I thought of Jack and the sweet tea he had given me in that railway waiting room in the middle of that vast desert. Had I really visited that place? Or had I simply been dreaming like Potter said I had been?

"Take a look at these," Potter said.

I glanced up to see him pulling a beige envelope from his coat pocket. He fished out two black and white photographs and handed them to me. I looked down at them. They appeared to be x-ray type images of a human skeleton. "Where did you find these?"

"In Ravenwood's study back at Hallowed Manor," Potter said, sitting down next to me before the fire. The flames reflected in his black eyes as he looked at me. "You told me that before Ravenwood died he said something about being able to hear the wind in the willows. Well, my trip back to Hallowed Manor didn't go exactly as planned and I had to hide in Ravenwood's office. It was while I was in there that I saw the book – you know – that kids' book, *The Wind in the Willows.* Knowing he had once left you a message in the same book in another *where* and *when*, I thought I'd check it out. Besides, the book stood out like a sore thumb on the bookshelf."

"How come?" I asked.

"All the other books were medical journals, physic books, and other such bollocks," Potter said, lighting a cigarette from the flames that twitched and jigged before us. "I couldn't find any kind of clue in the book but behind the bookshelf I found a small safe set into the wall. There was a lock where a key would have fitted – the key that Ravenwood gave you as he lay dying in the woods would have fitted it perfectly, I'm sure. Knowing you had the key, I busted the safe open and those pictures are what I found, along with some notes in the envelope. The notes would suggest that prior to the other Potter biting Sophie and turning her, Ravenwood undertook some tests on Sophie – perhaps to make sure that she was in good health or that she would even be able to cope with being turned. It appears that Ravenwood used that odd-looking camera of his to take some internal photographs of her, and it was while looking at them at a later date he must have realised that she wasn't pregnant. Take a look – can you see any signs of a baby?"

I glanced down at the pictures Potter had handed to me. There was no foetus in them. Sophie hadn't been pregnant with Potter's baby like she had claimed to be. "But why lie about something like that?"

"To get the other me to turn her – make her immortal," Potter said. "That's why Ravenwood tried to kill her because he found out what she was up to."

"But why didn't he just tell Murphy and the others what

he had found out?" I asked. "It doesn't make sense. He didn't have to try and kill her. He could have simply exposed her lie."

"Maybe there was another reason that he couldn't turn to the others for help," Potter said, before taking another puff of his cigarette. "I think the other Potter was keeping secrets too."

"What makes you think that?" I asked, handing him back the photos.

"Sophie cornered me on my way out of the manor," Potter said, placing the photographs back into the envelope. He then tossed it into the fire. "She thought I was her Potter. I think she wanted to have some jiggy-jiggy, but when I refused she got as mad as hell and accused me of having sex with you. I managed to break away and hide from her. She shouted that if I didn't come out she would reveal Potter's secrets. And I don't think she was talking about my love for you."

"She accused me of having sex with that other Potter too when she found me in the woods," I said.

Slowly, Potter turned his head to look at me. "Why would Sophie have thought such a thing if you and this other Potter were just friends?"

I frowned back at him. "What are you trying to say?"

"It's not what I'm saying – it's something Murphy said."

"What did he say?"

With his black eyes still fixed on mine, Potter said, "He said that you and Potter were close…"

"We were friends, that's all," I insisted, feeling suddenly affronted by his questions. "If you want to know if I found him attractive – of course I did. If you want to know whether I could have easy fallen in love with him – the answer is yes. Why wouldn't I want to fall in love with a man who was identical to you in every way? I couldn't just switch my feelings off. But I did fight them. The other you started to develop feelings for me. He went from zero to a million miles an hour within the space of a few days. At first I thought he didn't like me very much – just like you didn't when I arrived in the Ragged Cove. But he soon started to say that his feelings for me were changing. He said that it was like there was another side to him that he didn't know existed – a side of him that had always loved me. I thought that perhaps he really was you and that you had simply forgotten me just like Noah said you would. But either way it didn't matter to me because in this *where* and *when* you were with Sophie and I would've never come between that. However much it broke my heart, I had *pushed* you away. That was a decision I had made – it was a decision that, however uncomfortable, I knew I had to live with. So nothing happened between me and the other *you* – despite what Murphy thinks or says."

Potter looked away and into the fire. There was no apology for the unfounded insinuations he had just made. "What about this Nev? I heard that you went on a date with him."

"Oh, fuck you, Potter," I said, scrambling to my feet. "I don't have to sit here and listen to this."

Potter jumped up and stood before me. "I just want to know, were you and this Nev guy more than just friends?"

"How dare you even ask me that," I said, rolling back my fist and driving it squarely into Potter's face.

"Ouch!" Potter groaned, covering his blooded nose with one hand. "Why do you always do that?"

"Because you're a jerk, that's why!" I stormed away. "How can you ask me something like that...?"

"Murphy said..."

"I don't care what Murphy said!" I shouted at him, fists clenched at my sides. "If Murphy told you I'd become a freaking hooker would you have believed him?"

"Of course not," Potter said, wiping blood from his top lip.

"Why not?" I yelled. "You've already got me tagged with sleeping with the other Potter and Nev. Who else am I supposed to have dropped my knickers for? Ravenwood? Hunt? Murphy himself perhaps? How could you think such things of me? How dare you think such things about me after your track record?"

"What's that s'posed to mean? I haven't slept with any of those guys and I could hardly have had sex with myself..."

"I'm not talking about Murphy and the others, dick-head!" I shouted. "Eloisa Maddison, Sophie Harrison – do I need to go on?"

"No," Potter said, mopping the last of the blood from his nose.

"You really have no idea, do you?" I scowled with a shake of my head.

"About what?" he asked.

"About anything," I sighed in frustration.

"I found those pictures that Ravenwood left for you to find," Potter said with some kind of pride. "I figured that out."

"Whoopee-doo," I said, folding my arms across my chest and staring out across the valley. "Perhaps you could spend some of your time trying to figure me out, Potter."

"I know I love you more than I've ever loved anyone," he said, the anger fleeing his voice. "I know that's why I can't bear the thought of you loving another man even if he is my identical twin. That's why I risked everything to be with you, Kiera. That's why I gave up all my other friends to come and find you..."

"You have friends?" I sniped, unable to forgive him just yet.

"Of course I've got friends. There's Murphy, Kayla, Isidor... okay, there's Murphy," Potter conceded. "Although I doubt that he would ever forgive me if he knew what I'd done to his doppelganger in this *where* and *when*."

"What did you do?" I said, glancing back over my shoulder at him. "You didn't rip his heart out like you did Sophie's, did you?"

"No, I didn't kill him, although I guess that by now he probably wishes that I did," Potter said.

"Why?" I said, turning fully to face him.

"I handcuffed Murphy naked to a bed, stuffed a gag into his mouth, and left him in the capable hands of Mrs. Payne," he said, a smile threatening at the corners of his mouth as he stood looking at me from the other side of the cave.

"You did what?" I said, trying to fight the urge to smile myself. I didn't want to smile just yet. I wanted to stay mad at Potter a while longer. He deserved it.

"I bet she's eaten him alive by now," Potter said, that smile of his widening. "Gobbled him all up…"

"Yeah, thanks," I said, my own smile broadening. "Please spare me the grisly details. I'll be having nightmares for months."

Potter came slowly toward me. Stopping short of touching distance – was he scared I was going to punch him again? – he said, "I'm sorry, Kiera. I really am. I never meant to hurt you." He took a step closer still. "And I'm sorry I missed your birthday."

"That was my fault – if I hadn't have *pushed* you away then perhaps you would have been there," I said, easing up on him a little. Not all of this was Potter's fault.

"I know it's late, but I want to give you a birthday present," he said, reaching into his coat pocket.

"What is it?" I smiled.

Potter opened his hand to reveal his mother's ring. "I want you to have it."

Potter is going to give you a ring, I heard Jack whisper into my ear. *The ring once belonged to his mother. How would your daughter, Cara Hudson, have known this if you hadn't told her?*

"I couldn't possibly take it," I said, taking a step backwards, my heart suddenly racing. "It means too much to you."

"That's why I want you to have it," Potter said, taking my left hand in his. Slowly, he sank onto one knee before me. He looked up into my eyes as he slid the ring onto my left index finger. "I know I've asked you this once before, but I'm on my knees asking you again. Will you marry me, Kiera Hudson?"

I took a deep breath. "Yes," I whispered, staring down at the ring that Potter had just placed onto my finger.

Chapter Sixteen

Potter

Still on one knee before Kiera, I let go of her hand. I loosened the belt about her waist and slowly undid her jeans. As I eased them over her hips, along with her underwear, they slid to the ground. With her eyes locked with mine, Kiera stepped out of them, took off her coat and hoodie, and stood naked before me. Getting to my feet, I too removed all of my clothes. Taking her hand once again in mine, I led her slowly back across the cave toward the fire. Closing my wings and arms about her, I laid Kiera down on the ground before the writhing flames. She pressed the side of her face against my chest and I wished that the both of us could stay locked in the embrace for evermore.

"I love you, Kiera," I whispered.

"I love you more," she said, planting the softest of kisses against my chest.

Snaking my arms about her waist beneath our wings, I pulled her closer still, pressing my body against Kiera's as I kissed her. The flames cracked and snapped at our feet as the last of the sun faded and the moon rose over the valley outside. It felt as if we owned the world – as if it belonged to us and that we were the only two souls living in it. And for now that's what I wanted – Kiera was all that I wanted. Just the two of us together away from those who would want to hurt us and cause us pain. In my heart though, I felt that more pain was coming – there were more secrets to unravel and the truths that we discovered would only bring further heartache for the both of us. So for now, I wanted to shut such premonitions out – I wanted to forget the world and the pain in it and be with Kiera. Be one with the woman I hoped I would now spend the rest of eternity with.

As if being able to read my mind, or perhaps we had become so close that our feelings were becoming ever more in tune with each other, Kiera whispered, "Make love to me."

Not saying a word, I lay Kiera back in my arms. She closed her eyes, a dreamy expression pulled down over her face.

With my heart beginning to race in my chest as it always did when I was like this with Kiera, I began to cover every part of her face in featherlike kisses. I kissed the fast fading bruises that surrounded her eyes like stains. I kissed away the scratches that ran the length of one cheek, and the cuts that lined the curve of her neck. I flicked the tip of my tongue over the split in her bottom lip and her tongue came out to meet mine. I kissed her a little more deeply but not too much – not yet – that would come later. Easing my lips from over hers, I kissed her neck once more and I felt her shudder in my arms. Leaning just above her, our limbs entwined like a knot that could never be unravelled, I saw Kiera's soft flesh break out in gooseflesh as I began to gently smother her breasts then stomach in kisses. I took my time, relishing the smell of her skin and its smooth texture.

"I never want this to end," I whispered, my breath blowing warm against her skin.

"It doesn't have to," Kiera said back, her voice low and soft. She arched her back slightly. "We'll someday soon be married and nothing will then ever part us again."

I so wanted Kiera's words to come true, but still that sense of disquiet gnawed away at the back of my mind. Was it the wolf who was putting such doubts there? I didn't think so. The wolf was silent. I didn't want the wolf to invade these precious moments that Kiera and I shared. So I pushed any doubts that our future together might not be a happy one from my mind. I pushed it away like I did the wolf. Every moment I spent kissing Kiera – every moment we now shared together I wanted to be ours and ours alone.

I brushed my lips over Kiera's thighs, working my way down the length of her legs. I kissed every inch of them. I kissed her toes and she released a series of soft giggles as she wiggled her toes back and forth.

"Easy, tiger." I smiled along the length of her body at her.

"It tickles," she smiled, eyes half closed.

Raising her arms and reaching for me, I took hold of her hands and let her pull me down over her. I felt her ease her legs apart and I sunk between them so that we could become one again. Wrapping her arms about my shoulder, Kiera pulled me closer still. I felt her claws sink into my back and her fangs glistened in the glow of the fire that warmed the cave and us.

I moved slowly at first, working my hips back and forth in deep, deliberate thrusts. Kiera arched her back once more and murmured. Dragging her claws from the groove in my arse and up the length of my back to my shoulders, Kiera placed her lips over mine. She kissed me, but I knew that it wasn't my lips that she truly wanted. She traced the tip of her tongue from my lips, around my jawline, and down my neck. It was the red stuff that pumped beneath the flesh that she wanted so much. I felt the tips of her fangs pierce my skin as she formed a tight seal about the puncture wounds with her lips. She began to drink as I felt my blood pump into her mouth. Feeling Kiera's need for me – for all of me – only heightened my sense of pleasure and I began to work my hips harder and faster. Drinking each other's blood as we made love only brought the act to a deep intimacy that I had only ever felt and experienced with Kiera. And as I moved faster and faster over her, I could feel and smell the scent of Kiera's blood pumping at speed through her veins. I released a deep throaty sigh as the smell of her blood just beneath her flesh became maddening. Unable to fight the urge to taste it – feed from her – became as unbearable as the intoxicating throb I felt between my own thighs as I pushed myself deeper and deeper into her. With Kiera's hips bucking beneath me, I crushed my lips over the side of her neck and broke the skin there with my fangs. Her blood gushed into my mouth and down the back of my throat. I gulped it down in thick, hot, crimson streams as I continued to make love to her. Kiera continued to rake her claws up and down the length of my back as we moved together on the cave floor, wings and limbs entwined. To be like this together, drinking each other's blood, our bodies locked, we shared more than just each other's willing flesh – something far deeper than that. We shared our hopes, joys, fears, anguish, dreams, nightmares but most of all we shared a deep and unbreakable love for each other.

    I felt Kiera slide her fangs from my neck and roll her head back. She cried out as her body trembled beneath mine. With my own lips glistening with Kiera's blood, I arched my back, wings spreading wide as my own body began to rock and buck as if seized by a series of violent spasms. And despite the fact that this feeling now rocked my body like something close to agony, I wanted it to last forever. As Kiera continued to tremble beneath me, I held her tight in my arms. Just as my own, I could feel Kiera's heart pounding as our chests hitched up and down as we both gasped for breath. Collapsing in her arms, we stayed joined as one long after our lovemaking had ended.

Chapter Seventeen

Kiera

Taking Potter's face gently in my hands, I kissed my blood from his lips. I could see a thin trickle of blood streaming from the puncture marks I had left in his pale flesh. With my thumb, I wiped the blood away. It still felt warm to touch so I mopped it up with the tip of my tongue.

Smiling at me, Potter rolled onto his back. I watched his broad chest rise up and down. I watched how the flames from the nearby fire illuminated his strong-featured profile. How could someone who looked so rugged and masculine be such a tender and giving lover when he wanted to be? His hands were the size of shovels but there were times when he touched me where they felt as light as feathers. Reaching for his discarded jeans, Potter pulled out a pack of cigarettes and lit one. With his eyes closed, he blew smoke up into the air.

Propping myself up on one elbow so I could look down at him as he lay and smoked, I pulled one of my wings over us to keep warm. I ran my fingertips over his chiselled chest, and even though I could feel the thrum of his heart, I couldn't help but wonder how much of this was real.

"Is any of this real?" I asked him.

Opening one eye, he looked at me. "What we just shared certainly felt real enough. It nearly blew my fucking mind."

I shook my head at him. "No, I didn't mean that. What I mean is are *we* real?"

Potter opened both eyes now and looked up at me. "I'm not sure what you mean?" He drew deeply on his cigarette, the end of it glowing nearly as bright as the fire.

"Are we the real deal – are we the real Kiera and Potter?"

Potter frowned back at me. I could tell his brain was working overtime.

"What about the Potter from this *where* and *when*, he believed he was real, right?" I said.

"I guess," Potter said thoughtfully. "Look, where is this going?"

"He believed that he was real – that he was the real Potter and he was – to him he was," I said. "To the Sophie of this layer, the other Potter was very real. To them we are the imposters, and who says they aren't right?"

"I say," Potter said. "There's no one else like me and you, tiger."

"Don't you see that there is?" I said, sitting up, pulling my wings tight about me against the chill night wind that was now wailing through the valley. Potter continued to lay naked by the fire, seemly unaffected by the cold, and smoked. "There was another you here, another Murphy, Kayla, Isidor, Ravenwood, and others. What makes their lives any less real than ours?"

"But they're not us," Potter said. "And besides, most of them are dead now, anyway."

"Thanks to us," I said.

"It wasn't me that killed Kayla and Isidor, it was that double-crossing wolf, Lilly Blu."

"But I killed Potter and you killed Sophie," I said. "What right did we have to do that?"

"Sophie was going to kill you if I hadn't have stepped in," Potter reminded me.

"But if I hadn't have been here than she wouldn't have

almost been able to kill me," I said. "She would have married Potter..."

"That poor sod," Potter said, flicking the butt of his cigarette into the fire. Then kneeling up, he took the two skinned rabbits that had been cooking over the flames. He handed one to me. "It looks like you did him a favour by ripping his throat out, otherwise he might have spent the rest of his life with that lying cow, Sophie..."

"This isn't funny," I said, picking at the meat he had given me with my fingernails.

"Who's laughing?" Potter said, popping a piece of the rabbit meat into his mouth. "Sophie lied to him. And that's how I know the Potter from this layer wasn't real – wasn't *me*."

"How can you be so sure?"

"Because I wouldn't have fallen for Sophie's lies," he said around a mouthful of the meat. "I'm too switched on to be fooled by someone like her."

"Really?" I half smiled to myself.

"What's that s'posed to mean?"

"Nothing," I said, still smiling.

Tearing another strip of meat free from the bone, Potter said, "You were right about Murphy."

"How come?"

"He might look like my friend, but he wasn't him," Potter said. "He did kill Lilly Blu and he said that he did it because he discovered her murdering Kayla and Isidor – but I still don't believe the real Murphy would have killed her for that – however much he might have wanted to. Murphy loves Lilly Blu. Fuck knows why, but he does. He couldn't have ripped her head off no matter what she might have done."

I picked another strip of meat free, but I didn't have any appetite for it. I had a nagging feeling at the back of my mind and I didn't know quite what it was. But it made me feel uneasy. Placing the unfinished meat to one side, I said, "That night we made love..."

"Which one? There has been so many." Potter winked at me.

"The night before we went down into Snake Weed with the wolves led by Bruce Scott to confront Luke – we made love in that little cottage where we were hiding out with Murphy and the others. Do you remember it?" I asked him.

"Yeah, I remember it."

"Well, you told me that Noah had *pushed* you back through the cracks to go in search of the photographer. He sent you to a time in that layer before we'd been *pushed* into it, right?"

Potter nodded. "Right. So what?"

"You told me that you met another Kiera there," I reminded him. "At the time I said I didn't want to know about her because she wasn't me, but I've changed my mind. I'd like to know what she was like."

"Look, Kiera, no good will come of it," Potter said, tossing the rabbit's carcass into the fire, then licking his greasy fingers clean. "That was all in the past – in a different *where* and *when*."

"I would still like to know."

"Why?"

"What was she like?" I asked, unflinching.

"She was just like you," Potter sighed. "What more can I say?"

"You're hiding something from me, I can tell."

"You're becoming paranoid," Potter said, snatching up his jeans and jumping to his feet. He pulled the jeans up over his legs and zipped them up. I watched him search the cave for his boots.

"How was she like me?" I asked, getting up and putting on my clothes.

"She was a cop, okay? She drove a shitty red Mini like you do."

"What happened to her?" I asked, pulling on my coat.

Potter looked at me, his eyes dark and wide. It was like there was more but he just couldn't find the words to tell me.

"What is it? What happened?"

"Kayla blew the other Kiera's brains out," Potter sighed. "Happy now?"

"Kayla killed her?" I frowned. "Why?"

"Because Kiera was going to kill me."

"Kill you?"

"The other Kiera had already killed the Potter from that time," he said. "Luke had been using her just like he'd been using everyone else."

"Using how?"

"Look, Luke arrived in that layer ahead of us – you know that," he said, taking another cigarette and lighting it. Potter looked suddenly uncomfortable like there was something he didn't really want to tell me. "So he went looking for us to seek revenge. He found you first and you were living with me – we were both cops – just like before. To prove that you were loyal to him, he made you kill me while he watched."

"But why would the other me – the other *Kiera* – wanted to have been loyal to Luke Bishop?" I asked.

"Because the wolves in that layer thought that Luke Bishop was their leader – king of the Lycanthrope – the Wolf Man and the Kiera from that layer was a wolf..."

"A wolf?" I said, placing one hand to my face.

"She was a Vampyrus too – she had these little bony stumps sticking out of her back. It was like she was more wolf than Vampyrus, just like you're more Vampyrus than wolf..."

"She was a half and half like me," I said, trying to make

sense of what I was hearing.

"So what?" Potter shrugged. But despite his show of indifference I knew that he knew it was important – important to me at least.

"What you've told me only goes to prove what I've feared all along."

"And what's that?"

"Who are we to say that we're the real Kiera and Potter?" I said.

"Because you're standing here and the other Kiera is dead," Potter reminded me.

"But she had a life – she was a cop and living with you. As far as that Kiera was concerned she was very real – she was the one and only Kiera Hudson."

"Well it's not as if another Kiera or Potter is going to turn up here..."

"But why not?" I cut in. "We turned up in their layer. If the other Kiera you met was a half and half then she'd lived a life very much like mine. One of her parents must have been a wolf and the other a Vampyrus. We know that those children don't live – that I'm the only one who has – or so we first thought. Don't you see how all of our lives are very similar to those other versions of us?"

"But there is still no way another Kiera and Potter are going show up in this layer – we've already seen to that..." Potter started.

"But what about Kiera?" I broke in.

"You've lost me?" Potter frowned again.

"We've met the Potter, Murphy, Ravenwood, Hunt, and we know that Kayla and Isidor are dead... but what about the Kiera from this layer? We haven't met her? Where is she?"

"There might not be a Kiera Hudson in this layer – other

than the gorgeous one standing right in front of me," Potter said, cracking a smile.

"It's not a laughing matter, Potter," I said. "It could be important?"

"Important to what – to whom?"

"To me and the other Kiera," I said, heading for the cave entrance.

Potter gripped my arm and spun me around to face him. "Where are you going?"

"To find the Kiera Hudson from this *where* and *when*."

"Why? What's the point?"

"Because Potter from this layer is dead, so is Sophie, Ravenwood, Kayla and Isidor, too. Perhaps someone wants them all dead - perhaps they want the other me dead, too."

"But why?"

"I don't know. I've yet to find that out, but in the meantime, I must try and warn her," I said, pulling my arm free of Potter's grip and leaving the cave.

"And what's your plan?" Potter scoffed, catching up with me as I headed down into the valley. "You're just going to knock on her front door and introduce yourself as her long, lost identical twin? Are you hoping she's just going to invite you in for tea? And what are you going to say? Besides, she could live anywhere in this layer..."

"She'll live in Havensfield. She'll live in the rented rooms where I once lived." Scowling at Potter, I quickly added, "And she'll drive a shitty old Mini."

Before he'd had the chance to argue the point any further with me, I was springing up into the night, my wings humming on either side of me.

Chapter Eighteen

Potter

Deep down I thought that Kiera was wrong to go in search of her other self from this *where* and *when*. But hey, when did she ever fucking listen to me? Kiera was the most resourceful and headstrong woman I'd ever met and I guessed that was just one of the many things that I loved about her. She didn't take any shit – least of all from me. So rolling back my shoulders, I released my wings and shot up into the night sky after her. It wasn't long before two thunderous booms nearly tore the night in half.

We raced along next to each other, our wings angled back, England once again looking like nothing more than a blur way below. And although I was heading for Havensfield with Kiera, I still had deep misgivings about what she had decided to do. Although I was aware of the other Potters in different *wheres* and *whens* I wasn't sure that I would like to meet one of them. Christ, two of us at once would be more than I could handle. And I wasn't so sure that I wanted to know what kind of life the other me had led. I hadn't wanted to know that one version of me had planned to marry Sophie and not Kiera. Lilly had told me that Sophie and I had a daughter named Abbie. Had I put a stop to that ever happening now that Sophie in this layer was dead? But she hadn't really been pregnant. It had been a lie to trap, or in some way, deceive the other me. But if that wasn't going to happen now because the Potter and Sophie from this *where* and *when* were now dead, how had I seen the little girl named Abbie that Lilly Blu had said was my daughter? How had she haunted me in that layer

Noah had *pushed* me into? Perhaps there was a Potter and Sophie running around in some other layer playing happy families with a daughter named Abbie. But that wasn't my life and not the life for me – just like the life of the Kiera we had now gone in search of wasn't Kiera's life to live or influence. Her life was separate from that of the Kiera I loved. Even if their two lives did share some similarities, their lives were different – *they* were different. I wasn't so sure that I cared how many different versions of me were out there or if I was the genuine article or not. All I cared about now was the future life that I planned on sharing with Kiera – my Kiera. But perhaps Kiera could *see* something that I couldn't. Some future danger lying in wait for us. Something that might destroy us. That was what Kiera was good at – she saw stuff way before anyone else did.

Kiera swooped around in a wide loop and I banked with her. My coattails billowed around my legs and the collar of my coat flapped against the sides of my face. With her arms tucked into her sides and wings beating on either side of her, Kiera slowed and peered way below. As if finding her bearings, she shot forward, soaring out of the sky toward the twinkling lights of Havensfield that lay below. I dropped with her, the rush of wind making my cheeks and wings ripple. With dust flying up from beneath our boots, we thudded down into the small alleyway that was opposite the house with the rented rooms where Kiera had once lived. I didn't need Kiera to point out the beat-up old Mini that was parked at the curb on the other side of the street, but she did anyway.

"Okay, smartarse, you were right about the car but I still think you're wrong about this whole thing," I said.

"We'll *see*," Kiera said stepping out of the alleyway and into the street.

I followed her across the quiet street to the steps that led up to the front door of the rented rooms that Kiera had once rented – in some other layer, I reminded myself. I glanced sideways and could see that Kiera had stopped in front of the red Mini. It was scratched and dented as much as her own. She reached out and stroked the bonnet.

"For Christ's sake, Kiera, it isn't a fucking cat."

"Me and this car have been through a lot," Kiera said.

"It isn't *your* car," I reminded her. Taking her by the arm, I dragged her away from the piece of junk and onto the pavement.

"I thought you'd come to find the other Kiera, not admire her car," I said, trying to bring her back to reality.

"My car," she muttered under her breath, heading for the door of the house.

I followed her up the stone steps, where Kiera was now rattling the lock. The door was stuck fast. Easing her aside, I punched out my claws and raised them.

"No," she whispered, taking hold of my wrist.

I watched her reach into her coat pocket from which she produced a keyring. She sifted through the keys that hung from it. Then taking the one she wanted, she slid it into the lock. Before twisting the key, she looked at me. "I wonder?" she said, before turning the key.

There was an audible click as the lock opened. Raising her eyebrows at me, and a know-it-all smile creeping around the edges of her lips, Kiera pushed open the door and stepped inside the building where she had once – in another *where* and *when* – lived.

Chapter Nineteen

Kiera

It felt strangely familiar to be back in the house where I had rented rooms. It seemed like several lifetimes ago – but it still somehow felt like home to me. Even though it was dark in the hallway, I could see that it was decorated with the same floral wallpaper and carpeted with the same garish purple coloured rug. With Potter at my heels, I made my way to the foot of the stairs that led up into darkness and the rooms where I had spent so many hours sitting in my favourite chair by the window and watching the world pass by below. Before placing one foot down on the stairs, I felt Potter put one hand onto my shoulder.

"It's not too late for you to change your mind, Kiera. It's not too late to turn back."

"Turn back to what? Go where?" I said over my shoulder at him. "We don't belong here. This isn't our layer."

"Then why are we snooping about?" he asked. "What good can it do? We'd be better off trying to figure out a way of getting back to our friends where I left them waiting by the fountain."

"You said there was no way back," I reminded him as I started to climb the stairs. "You told me that's what Lilly Blu said."

"She's said plenty of stuff that hasn't exactly worked out to be true," Potter said.

"I can't just let the Kiera from this layer come to harm because I've been pushed into it," I said.

"Who says she's going to come to any harm?" Potter said,

climbing the stairs behind me. Besides she..."

"Shhh!" I said raising one hand. "Look, the door to my rooms – to *her* rooms – is ajar."

"So perhaps she popped out to get a pint of milk or something," Potter suggested.

I glanced over my shoulder at him. "What, at three o'clock in the morning?"

"Perhaps..."

"What's that smell?" I cut over him.

"I don't smell anything?"

And even though Potter couldn't, I could and I knew that I had smelt it before. It was the smell of death from a body that had started to decay and spoil. I'd come across the same smell when discovering young Henry Blake's corpse lying torn to pieces beneath the tree in the Ragged Cove. I had taken little notice of what Potter had said then as he'd scoffed at the remarks about what I had *seen* at the crime scene. And I ignored him now, as I reached the top stair and slowly pushed open the door that led into the room. The smell of rotting flesh was so pungent that I placed one hand over my nose and mouth. I stood stock still in the open doorway – unable to step into the room. Seeing myself sitting in the chair with my head thrown back, eyes and mouth wide open was startling enough, but it was the angry black and red hole in the centre of my forehead that made my stomach lurch. To see myself sitting dead in my favourite armchair with a bullet hole in my face made my stomach lurch and knees turn weak. Stepping up behind me, Potter took one look over my shoulder and said, "Kiera you don't need to see this. It isn't right..."

"But I was right, wasn't I?" I said, my words coming out in breathless gasps. "I knew she was in danger... why hadn't I *seen* it sooner?"

"No one can see everything all of the time, not even you," Potter said softly, as if trying to offer me some comfort. "What happened here isn't your fault."

"No, but I'm going to find out who's fault it is," I said, trying to gather myself together.

"How? It could have been anyone," Potter said.

"I'm going to do what I do best," I said, crouching low and beginning to inspect the floor. I brushed my fingertips over the carpet, the tip of my nose just inches from it. Standing up and spinning around, I began to inspect the door for clues. "Stand over there," I said to Potter.

He moved to one side.

"Not there, there!" I instructed him. "You're blocking the light from the street lamp."

"Why not just turn the light on?" Potter said, reaching for the light switch.

"No!" I said, jabbing my forefinger in the air at him. "Don't touch anything!"

"Okay, sor-reey," Potter groaned, skulking to the furthest corner of the room. I heard him dig the packet of cigarettes out from his coat pocket. I glared back at him. Without saying a word, he pushed the cigarette back into the packet then into his pocket. He folded his arms across his chest and sulked.

I turned my attention back to the room. First, I inspected the door. I ran my fingers over the lock and frame. When I'd seen enough, I turned around and faced the dead *me* sitting in the chair with the gaping bullet wound in her face. With my hands on my hips I surveyed the scene. I looked at the dried blood, brain and partial skull fragments that had dried to the wall behind the chair. Springing across the room, I went to the wall. I looked at the dried gunge then down at Kiera. With great care, I took hold of her head in my hands and slowly eased it forward. Her neck felt brittle and stiff – like I was handling a statue. Taking a deep breath as her flesh had started to smell real bad, I leaned in and studied the bullet wound in the back of her head. When I was satisfied, I leant her back in the position in which I had found her. I then circled the chair and looked down at her. It seemed too surreal to be looking at myself dead in the armchair where I had spent so many hours sitting. But it wasn't me sitting in that chair, I kept telling myself over and over. With that thought at the forefront of my mind, I leaned into her so our noses were almost touching. Her skin had started to turn green in places and blisters had started to form about her lips, under her chin, and along her neck. It was where the fluid in her body was starting to pool and congeal. I stared into her black eyes. The whites had gone yellow. Reaching out, I gently closed the lids over them.

Stepping back from the chair, I gently took hold of her hands. Her wrists made a snapping noise as I lifted them. Her hands felt stiff and brittle in mine. I looked closely at her fingernails. When I had seen enough, I placed her hands back in her lap. The dead Kiera was dressed in her dressing gown and it was secured about her waist. Her feet were bare. Kneeling down, I inspected them by checking the soles and toenails. Placing her feet back down, I noticed something beneath the chair. It was an envelope. I picked it up and took out the letter that was folded up inside. I read it. I read it again. I turned it over in my hands, then tucked it into my coat pocket. Standing up, I crossed to the other side of the room where an ironing board had been erected. A blouse hung from a hanger that had been fixed to the back of the door. I glanced down and saw a pair of shoes. I picked them up and inspected the heel and soles. Content that I was getting a measure of things, I placed the shoes back where I had found them and went to the bedroom. The room was nearly identical to how I had once had it. The only thing that was missing was a picture of me and my father that I'd always kept on the windowsill. I looked at the bed and knew that I had seen enough. I returned to the living room and looked at Potter.

"Well?" he asked. "What have you seen?"

"Kiera knew her killer for starters," I said, "and was let into the room by her. Seconds later the killer produced a gun. Kiera turned and was shot in the back of the head. The killer then placed her in the chair and left."

"But it looks like she was sitting down, how do you know that she let the killer in? And from the way she's sitting and all the shit up the wall, it looks to me as if she was shot in the face, not in the back of the head," Potter said, stepping from the corner of the room and into the beam of street light that poured in through the window.

"Ah, we were just meant to think that," I said. "The killer wanted to make it look like she was shot by a complete stranger. But I know Kiera let her killer in – she knew whoever it was."

"How can you be so sure?" Potter asked me.

"She was killed in the evening, when it was dark…" I started.

"Really?"

"Blood is smeared on the light switch by the door," I told him. "The killer turned the light out as he or she left. If the crime had taken place during the day, why had the light been switched on?"

"So how did the killer get blood on him if he shot her from the doorway?" Potter frowned.

"Like I said, Kiera let her killer in. And as it was night and she lived alone, there is no way that she would have let a stranger up – not if she was anything like me and we've got to presume that she was. The front door works on a buzzer system. Kiera would have asked who they were before they'd even got past the front door. No, whoever her killer was, he or she buzzed first. Recognising their voice Kiera let them in. She then went to the door. When he or she stepped into the room, it was then that Kiera saw they had a gun. As her killer took aim, Kiera turned and they shot her once in the back of the head. Once she was dead, the killer then lifted her up and sat her in the chair. That's how the murderer got blood on their hands."

"But she could have already sat down in the chair before the killer fired the gun," Potter said.

"Look here," I said, pointing to the hole in the centre of Kiera's face. "This is the exit wound. The entry wound is at the back of her head. She couldn't have been sitting down and shot in the back of the head or else the blood spatter would be on the floor and not up the wall. So all the facts suggest that she was standing up when she was shot in the back of her head by the killer. So therefore it could only have been the person who fired the gun who picked her up and placed her in the chair," I explained.

"How long has she been dead?" Potter asked.

"She was murdered on the night of the first of June," I said.

"How can you be so exact?" Potter asked.

"Because I was pushed into this *where* and *when* five days before my twenty-first birthday which was on the 6th of June," I told him.

"But I still don't see how you figured out she was murdered on the first of June?"

"Because she was attending an interview the following morning," I said, crossing the room to the ironing board. I pointed at the blouse hanging from the back of the door. "She had spent the day she was murdered preparing for a new job interview. She ironed her blouse and had gone and bought some new shoes." I pointed to the high heels that had been placed by her on the floor by the bedroom door. "The shoes show no signs of scuff marks and they still have the price label stuck to the sole. There is a skirt laid out on the bed too. She had a full manicure and pedicure the day of her killing too, I checked her hands and feet. No, she wanted the job – she was trying to make an impression."

"Wouldn't the people who sent her for the job interview have wondered why she didn't turn up for the job?" Potter asked.

"She did turn up for the job interview, Potter," I said, looking across the room at him. "I turned up."

"You've lost me..." Potter said, reaching for his smokes again, then thinking better of it.

"Don't you remember I told you how when I was *pushed* from that underground platform, I woke up to find myself in my car travelling back into the Ragged Cove?" I asked him. "There was a letter addressed to me on the passenger seat of my car asking me to attend an interview at the offices of The Creeping Men." I reached into my pocket and pulled out the same letter that I had found under Kiera's armchair. "This is an identical letter." I crossed the room to the blouse and the high heeled shoes. "These are identical shoes and clothes to what I was wearing when I woke to find myself heading back into the Ragged Cove."

Potter looked at me, a blank expression on his face.

"Oh, my God, Potter, don't you see?" I said, slapping my forehead with the palms of my hands. "This Kiera was killed in this *where* and *when* because whoever murdered her wanted me to attend that interview at the offices of The Creeping Men and not her."

"But why?" Potter said, eyes growing darker.

"That I don't know," I said, frustrated. "But I will find out, and when I do, I'll rip their heart out."

"Hey, it's not like you to get so angry – to want to kill anyone," Potter said, coming toward me.

"It is like me, Potter," I said, heart racing. I felt the sudden sting of tears in my eyes. "How are we ever going to have a life together? Get married," I said, waving the finger with the ring on it before him, "if we keep getting screwed like this? How are we ever meant to have a family – settle down and live a regular life just like anyone else? We don't stand a chance, Potter, unless we get to the bottom of this. I'm just so tired of running and fighting the whole time. I just want to be able to stop every once in a while and a take a look around, without having to keep glancing back over my shoulder the whole time."

I wanted to tell him that part of me believed that one day we might have a daughter named Cara – that we might have a chance of having a family and being happy. But how was that ever going to be possible if someone had other plans for me and him.

"Do you think the Elders are behind what's happened here?" Potter asked.

"No – I don't know," I sighed. "But I'm guessing that there is someone who might know."

"Who?"

"The White Wolf – Lilly Blu," I said, heading for the door.

"But she killed Kayla and Isidor," Potter said. "Do you think she killed you – murdered this Kiera, too?"

"I'm not sure of anything anymore," I said, heading out of the door. Then stopping, I peered around the edge of the door and back into the room to discover Potter reaching down for the pair of shiny black high heels.

"Don't you dare," I snapped at him.

"Oh, c'mon, Kiera," he sighed. "You'd look so hot..."

"Put them down and close the door behind you," I said, heading back down the stairs, leaving the other Kiera Hudson dead and decomposing behind me.

Chapter Twenty

Kiera

As I raced away from Havensfield and back toward the valley, I couldn't help but feel disturbed that the other Kiera Hudson had been dead and festering in those rented rooms since I myself had arrived in this *where* and *when*. Whoever had executed her had known that I was coming – that I was about to be *pushed* into this layer. But who knew and how did they know? Did even Noah truly know where I was going to end up after taking that train from the Grand Station? Was Noah in some way behind this? Couldn't I trust him, after all? But why then help me to defeat the Elders? I was no longer able to trust anyone – other than Potter.

I glanced sideways to see him soaring beside me. His tatty-looking wings were within touching distance of my own. Potter was staring front as the wind pulled his wild black hair back in messy clumps. He had a somewhat grim and determined look on his face. Was he pissed-off that I hadn't let him take the high heels? I smiled to myself and looked away. I was so glad that Potter was back with me – the real Potter – my Potter. He was infuriating at times but he was a glimmer of light in the darkest of situations. When my life became too dark, Potter knew how to cast some light into it and make me smile. I looked at the ring that had placed onto my finger. How had Jack known about it? Had my daughter – a child that Potter and I had yet to have – really told him about how I came by the ring? The thought of such a thing didn't scare me or freak me out. On the contrary, it filled my heart with hope. If what Jack had said was true and Potter and I did have a daughter named Cara, then it meant that we had some kind of future together. It meant that however bad life became for us, we somehow would find a way of figuring it out and survive long enough to get married, have a daughter, and raise her. It was a glimmer of hope that I now clung onto and I wasn't going to let it go without a fight. That's why it was so important for me to find the White Wolf – Lilly Blu – if that's who the wolf really was. I knew that Murphy had told Potter that he had found Lilly Blu murdering Kayla and Isidor – but like I'd said – I was no longer sure who to trust. Unless I heard Lilly Blu confess in her own words that it had been her who had murdered my friends then I was going to keep an open mind. I was going to look for the facts and see what I could *see*. If Lilly Blu and the White Wolf were the same entity, why then hadn't the wolf killed me in the valley? Why had it led me to that shack where I'd been joined with Potter again? Why had she led him to it? Why bring us back together? There had to be a reason.

Dropping my shoulder to the right, I banked in that direction and Potter followed. I could see the valley below and it looked like a deep craggy scar zigzagging its way through the hills and mountains below. I headed in the direction of where the shack stood. Nearing the end of the valley, I started to lose altitude, soaring out of the night sky in a blaze of fleeting black shadows. I landed hard, planting both feet down onto the hard-packed ground, sending up a cloud of dust. Potter landed just feet away, creating his own storm of debris. Lighting a cigarette, he looked at me then toward the shack that stood just feet away.

"Is this the place?" he asked, striding toward it.

"Don't you remember?" I asked.

"No, not really. I was being mind-fucked by a wolf at the time," he said, taking hold of the iron doorknob that protruded from the door. He yanked on it but the door wouldn't budge. He pulled on it harder still and the rickety shack tilted left and right. "The door is jammed or locked…"

"I don't think it's locked," I said, joining him at the door. "I don't think we're meant to open it."

"Why not?" Potter said, cigarette bobbing up and down in the corner of his mouth as he spoke.

"Maybe only wolves can open it," I said. "After all, this shack – this valley – has some kind of significance to the wolves in this *where* and *when*."

"We're both half wolf, aren't we?" Potter said, pulling on the handle again. "That's got to count for something or what's the fucking point?"

I eased his hand from the doorknob. "I think we're just going to have to wait."

"For what?"

"The white wolf, I guess," I said, turning and heading away from the shack. When I was several meters away from it, I sat down on the ground and crossed my legs and faced the door. The night had turned suddenly cold, so I pulled my hood up over my head and began my wait for the White Wolf. I watched Potter kick the wooden door of the shack, then come toward me. He sat just feet away, his arms folded across his chest, and collar of his coat turned up.

"Well this is fun," he muttered. "How long are we going to have to sit here?"

"I don't know," I said, sliding my hands into my coat pockets to keep warm.

"It's fucking freezing," he said. "Why has it got so cold all of a sudden? Do you think a storm is coming?"

"I think so," I said, looking up at the sky. But there were no clouds that I could see. The sky was black and filled with a million pinpricks of bright white light from the stars. I couldn't ever recall seeing such a clear and crisp night sky. And as I sat and looked up, shivering with the cold, it looked like it had started to move – shift forward at an incredible speed. The stars started to race across the black night above me like I was watching a time-lapse video.

"Potter, look," I whispered, pulling myself to my feet.

Potter glanced up, then sprang to his feet. "What the fuck?"

Together we turned around and around on the spot, heads tilted back as we stared up into the night sky. The stars blazed across it as if time was somehow being stretched.

"Is it some kind of storm?" Potter muttered, perhaps more to himself than me. "Is that the wind I can hear howling?"

"No, I don't think it's the howl of the wind you can hear," I said, turning my attention away from the sky above and looking back along the valley.

"What then?" Potter said, looking at me.

Slowly, I pointed to where the White Wolf now sat some distance away further along the valley.

Chapter Twenty-One

Kiera

"Hey! You!" Potter hollered at the wolf, his voice rebounding off the craggy walls that rose up on either side of us for as far as the eye could see.

At the sound of his voice, the White Wolf simply turned and sauntered away from us with a swish of its long bushy tail.

"Where's it going?" Potter said setting off at a pace after the wolf. "We can't let it get away.

"You won't catch it," I said, running after him.

"We'll see," Potter said, springing into the air and racing at speed just above the floor of the valley after the wolf. But no sooner had he taken to the air than the wolf had somehow warped ahead further still. The wolf seemed able to move as fast as the speeding stars above our heads.

"It's no use, you won't catch it," I said, drawing level with Potter. He lowered himself out of the air, landing next to me.

"Then what's the point of being here if we'll never catch up with it?" Potter groaned.

I looked into the distance to see that the wolf had stopped again. It sat on its giant haunches and stared back at us, its eyes burning like two glowing suns on the horizon. "It wants us to follow it," I said.

"Where to?"

I shrugged. "I don't know, but we won't find out standing here." I set off through the valley after the wolf. No sooner had I taken a few steps forward, the wolf set off again. Sauntering slowly forward, its tail whipped to and fro.

"It could be leading us into a trap," Potter said, catching up with me. "We don't know if we can trust it."

"We don't know anything," I said, keeping my eyes firmly set ahead on the wolf. "And that's why we must follow if we want to find out..."

"Find out what?" Potter asked over the sound of our boots crunching over gravel and stones.

"Who killed me in this layer," I said.

"We're following the killer right now, Kiera," Potter said.

"Best we don't lose her then," I said right back, striding out ahead.

"This isn't just about you..."

"No, it's about *us*," I said, glancing sideways at him. "Like I said before, I don't want us to keep running and fighting, Potter. I know there is a better life – a better future out there for us. A place where we can have the life that we both so want. A life where we're happy, where we have a family... we just need to find it, that's all."

"And you really think that this wolf – Lilly-fucking-Blu – will lead us to it?" Potter said.

"She brought us back together, didn't she? Why did she do that?"

"Who knows how her mind works."

"And that's why we need to follow, or what else do we do?" I asked. "Do we run for the hills and play at being happy? I've tried that, Potter. I tried it when I *pushed* you and all of my other friends away and it doesn't work. Sure, I kept telling myself that I was happy, but I wasn't – not really. How could I be? I didn't have you, Murphy, Kayla, or Isidor in my life. I'm nothing without you all. You're my family – we're a family and families are strongest when they stick together and don't break apart. I'm stronger when I'm with you all. And that's why I went on that date with Nev, it wasn't because I wanted to jump into bed with him. It was because I was so fucking lonely. It broke my heart to see you with Sophie, to know that you were getting married and having a child. It broke my heart because they were all the things I wanted to share with you. But you weren't you – you were someone else. You weren't mine. None of my friends here in this layer were my true friends. I have only ever known such loneliness once before and that was when my father died and I was left sitting in that armchair staring out of the window for days and nights on end. So when Nev invited me out for my birthday I was secretly delighted. It was my birthday and I couldn't bear to spend another one of them alone – staring out of the window."

"I'm sorry, Kiera," Potter said as we continued to follow the wolf through the valley.

"You don't have anything to be sorry for..."

"Yes I do," Potter said. "I accused you of..."

"Yeah and I *pushed* you away. I think it makes us even," I said. "But I know one thing for sure, both of us will be sorry if we don't find out the truth and let the future I know awaits us be destroyed."

"You sound like you know what the future holds for us," Potter said.

It was on the tip of my tongue to tell him everything that Jack had told me, but I bit my lip instead. What would be the point in talking of dreams and nightmares? Jack had told me once that it's not good to know too much about one's future – he said it could change things. And perhaps he was right. The knowledge that perhaps one day Potter and I would have a daughter named Cara had already changed my perspective – the actions that I now took – hadn't it? So looking at Potter, I said, "All I know for sure is that I want to spend the rest of my life with you."

We continued to follow the white wolf through the valley. After what seemed like an age, we came across the slaughtered remains of the wolves I had killed with the other Potter as we'd tried to rescue Nev.

"What the fuck happened here?" Potter said, stepping over the shredded limbs and decaying corpses of the wolves.

"We happened," I said. "Well, me and the other Potter that is."

"It looks as if he hated wolves as much as I do," Potter said, cigarette hanging from between his lips, smoke drifting from it.

"Perhaps more," I said, glancing in the direction where I had buried Nev. I couldn't see the mound of rocks that I had buried him under. Perhaps it had been further down the valley? Maybe I'd been so upset at the time that perhaps I'd forgotten where his grave now was?

The sky and the stars continued to race overhead like a mesmerizing blur as we followed the white wolf deeper into the valley. It stayed exactly the same distance from us, however fast or slow we walked. The night seemed to stretch out with no end. For how long we walked, I didn't know, but it seemed like days. But if our journey through the valley really had lasted that long, the sun never rose – it was just one long, continuous night. And all through that time, neither Potter nor I became tired, thirsty, or hungry.

When it seemed like I had completely lost track of time and all sense of direction, I looked up to see that the wolf was now standing atop of a granite rock that jutted from the side of the valley. The moon spun around and around in the night sky like a silver-plated Frisbee. The wolf's white fur shimmered in the moonlight. Throwing back its giant head, the wolf howled, then licked its long snout. Its brilliant orange eyes met mine. It woofed down at me and Potter then with a flick of its tail, the wolf set off again. But this time, the wolf headed out of the never-ending valley, scrambling up the rocks that formed the side of the valley.

I headed toward the rocks that the wolf was now climbing.

"Easy, tiger," Potter whispered, gripping my arm. "Be careful."

"I think I can climb a few rocks…"

"I wasn't talking about the rocks," Potter said. "We don't know what's on the other side of that ridge."

"There's only one way of finding out," I said, setting off over the rocks and up toward the ridge.

Potter scrambled up behind me without making any further comment. The climb wasn't steep and it wasn't long before I was just feet from the top. I looked up to see the wolf peering back down over the ridge at me. It yelped once, before turning and disappearing from view.

"C'mon," I said, looking back over my shoulder at Potter. He was staring up at my arse. He grinned at me. Rolling my eyes, I looked front and started to climb again.

Reaching the top of the valley, I scrambled up and onto my feet. Within moments, Potter was standing beside me. I brushed dust from off my hands and the seat of my jeans.

"Where are we?" Potter asked. "And where's the wolf?"

I stared ahead into the thick, lush forest the wolf had led us to. I peered amongst the maze of trees that now stood before us, but couldn't see any sign of the wolf. Cupping my hands around my mouth, I shouted, "Lilly Blu."

The sound that came back to me from deep within the forest wasn't a howl or a bark, but a gut-wrenching scream.

Chapter Twenty-Two

Potter

"What was that?" I asked Kiera.

Before she'd had a chance to answer, I saw what looked like a young girl go sprinting through the trees ahead of us. Kiera saw her too, and raced forward amongst the trees.

"Kiera!" I hissed. But it was too late, she was gone, racing away in the pursuit of the girl. "Oh, for fuck's sake," I groaned before setting off after her. Why couldn't Kiera just leave things alone? Weren't we up to our necks in shit already?

I raced between the skyscraper-tall tree trunks, keeping my eyes on Kiera, who was just feet ahead of me. "Kiera, wait up!" I called after her. "Maybe we should head back to the ridge. I thought we were meant to be following the wolf!" But my pleas for her to see reason fell on deaf ears as Kiera continued to race forward. I quickened my pace and drew level with her as we darted between the tree trunks that loomed up into the dark all around us.

"See!" Kiera said, pointing forward.

I peered ahead. "See what?"

"That young girl," Kiera said. "It was her who screamed."

"So what? It has nothing to do with us."

"She could be in danger," Kiera breathed, drawing in breath as she quickened her pace until she was little more than a blur beside me.

I matched her speed. "So? It's not our problem – we've got enough of our own."

Kiera suddenly stopped, a shower of dead leaves spraying up from beneath the heels of her boots. "We've lost her," she said, drawing breath.

"Good," I said. "Now perhaps we can go back and look for the wolf..."

"Shhh!" Kiera hissed, raising one hand and peering through the trees that surrounded us. It was dark and hot in the forest – almost claustrophobic. I think I preferred the chill of the valley. "Can you hear that?" Kiera asked, her voice barely a whisper.

"I can't hear anything," I said, not dropping the level of my voice at all. "I think we should head back..."

"Shhh," Kiera said again. Then nodding in the direction of a nearby tree, she whispered. "Over there."

"Over where?" I sighed. Kiera set off in the direction that she had nodded to. I reached for her, but she was gone too soon and my fingers barely brushed the sleeve of her coat. Reluctantly, and with my hackles up, I followed Kiera as she crept toward the tree. Within inches from it, that ear-splitting scream came again. I glanced up and looked in the direction that the cry had come from to see a winged creature dropping at speed from the branches above. I reached out, to push Kiera away, but wasn't fast enough. With wings beating furiously up and down, the creature dropped on Kiera, sending her sprawling into the dirt and earth that covered the forest floor. The bedraggled-looking creature raised what looked like a set of jagged claws. I shot forward and gripped its wrist. With one sharp tug, I pulled the creature free of Kiera and sent it spinning through the air into the nearest tree trunk. The creature cried out and dropped to the ground with a heart-stopping thud. I heard it hiss, and through the filthy hair that covered its face, I saw a set of drooling fangs and two dead black eyes.

Screaming, the creature sprang at me. With my claws breaking free of my fists, I snatched the winged beast out of the air. Now that I had hold of it, I could tell that the creature felt emaciated and was little more than a heap of brittle bones covered in a layer of flesh. However, it was strong and it wrestled against me as I tried to restrain it. The creature clawed, hissed, and spat at me like it was insane. Fearing that if it broke free it might kill Kiera or me – perhaps both – I raised one claw intending to put the wild creature out of its misery. I felt a hand grip my wrist.

"No, Potter!" Kiera shouted. I looked back to see that it was Kiera who had taken hold of my arm, stopping me from killing the frenzied creature. "Look, it's a Vampyrus. It's just a girl."

I glanced back at the creature, who was kicking wildly against my grip. And through the matted and untamed hair that hung over the creature's face, I could see that Kiera was right and it was a young girl.

"Let go of her," Kiera said.

"Why, so she can rip our throats out?" I said.

"She's just scared," Kiera said. Then peering past the dirty black hair that lay matted over the girl's face, she said, "You won't hurt us, will you?"

The girl screeched at Kiera like she didn't have any understanding of language. As if sensing this, Kiera shrugged her shoulders and unfurled her wings. She let them flap slowly on either side of her. "We're creatures just like you," Kiera said to the girl, who continued to struggle against me. "Me and my friend, Potter, are Vampyrus like you."

From behind the lengths of bedraggled hair that covered her face, I could see the girl look at Kiera's wings. Her dark eyes grew wide. It was like she had never seen a Vampyrus before, despite being one herself. The girl's struggles against me became less.

"We're not going to hurt you," Kiera said softly. "We just want to help you."

From behind her hair, the girl continued to stare at Kiera as I felt the fight slowly subside inside of her. Sensing that she was no longer a threat to either of us, I slowly eased my grip on her.

"See, we're not going to hurt you," Kiera smiled at her, her wings still humming behind her. "My name is Kiera Hudson. What's yours?"

The girl said nothing. She stepped away from both of us, as if keeping a safe distance – perhaps fearing that we could be a threat to her after all. Now that she was no longer fighting against me, I could see that the girl was about fifteen years of age – perhaps sixteen? It was so hard to tell with her hair masking much of her face. She wore a dress that I guessed must have once been white. But it was now a filthy grey and torn in several places. Her arms, claws, legs, and feet were covered in dirt.

She cowered before us. Noticing this, Kiera took a step toward her. The girl flinched away. Kiera stopped. "You don't have to be scared. Who were you running from?"

Raising one hand, and pointing back over our shoulders, the girl spoke for the first time and said in little more than a whisper, "I was running from them."

Turning around and looking in the direction that the girl was pointing, I raised my claws at the wolves that were racing out of the dark toward us.

Chapter Twenty-Three

Kiera

On seeing the wolves, Potter shot forward and so did I. The Lycanthrope came charging at us from between the trees that circled us on all sides. The young girl stumbled back – another shrill scream escaping her throat. I glanced back to see that her hair had now fallen away from the sides of her face. I had never seen such fear before. Looking forward again, I confronted the snarling wolf that was now lunging through the gloom at me. I slashed my claws at the giant hound, tearing open a hole in its throat. Blood splashed my face in hot jets as the wolf dropped to the floor. Another pounced forward to replace the one I had just killed. Potter was happily disembowelling one wolf with one claw while slitting the throat of another. The wolf's barks and howls were thunderous in the thick of the forest and branches shook over our heads as Potter swiped at the wolves, sending them flying back through the air and into the trees. But for every wolf we killed, another came charging out of the forest to attack us.

I leapt into the air, knowing that I would have the advantage over the wolves from above. But before I'd had the chance to take flight, one of the wolves had fastened its claw about one of my ankles. It snatched me out of the air, slamming me down hard on the forest floor. I cried out as the air exploded from my lungs. I glanced up to see several of the wolves coming toward me. They came from all sides. I was surrounded. But I knew that I couldn't give up or give in. Some of the wolves walked on two legs, others on all fours. Some of them looked semi human like I sometimes did when the wolf inside of me hadn't fully consumed me. But where was that wolf now? Why wasn't it chomping at the bit to come forward and help defend me against the wolves? Was that the reason? Wouldn't the wolf come forward if it meant killing its own kind? How could it pick and choose like that? Didn't the wolf understand that if I died, then so too did she? I searched my mind for it, but all I could see was my Vampyrus self, standing dead centre and front – her long blue hair billowing out from over her shoulders, fangs and claws out, black wings beating feverishly on either side of her.

Seeing her there, I sprang forward, claws raised, fangs searching for blood as I launched myself at the nearest wolf. One of its mighty claws connected with my jaw, snapping my head backwards and sending me pin-wheeling back through the air. I clattered into the nearest tree, causing a flurry of leaves to shower down from above.

"Stop your fight, Kiera Hudson," I heard one of the wolves roar.

How did any of them know who I was? I glanced up from the ground where I lay.

"And you, Potter," the voice boomed again.

Hearing his name spoken, Potter spun around, blood dripping from his fangs and entrails sliding from his claws. Both of us watched the werewolf who had spoken walk forward and toward us. He walked up right. He was as broad as a table, his arms and legs thickset. His dark brown hair and beard that lined the sides of his face was bushy and long. His eyebrows met over his fierce burning eyes. He wore a dark emerald tunic, coarse black trousers, and boots. A cloak hung about his shoulders. Both Potter and I recognised him at once. His name was Bruce Scott. Did he recognise us? Was that how he knew our names? Did he even have the faintest recollection that we had once fought alongside him in Snake Weed?

"Bruce Scott," Potter said.

"You've heard of me then?" Scott said in his booming voice.

"We know you… we fought alongside you in Snake Weed…" Potter started

"Lies," Scott said. "We have never met before."

And as if to punish Potter for his so-called lies, another of the wolves leapt forward and punched Potter squarely in the face. Potter dropped to his arse. No sooner had he hit the ground, Potter was up again, driving his claws through the air at the wolf who had just struck him.

"Stop or we kill the Vampyrus girl," Scott roared.

I glanced in the direction that I had last seen the fragile-looking girl to see that she was now the prisoner of a wolf who had its claws against her throat. I could see enough of the girl's face from behind her lanky hair to know that she was petrified.

"Kill her," Potter said. "She means nothing to me."

"No!" I shouted, scrambling to my feet. "Don't harm her."

I looked at Scott and him at me. There was no spark of recognition in his eyes. As far as he was aware, we had never met before. Or perhaps I was wrong. Tilting his head to one side, he came slowly toward me.

"So you're the real Kiera Hudson," he said, taking my chin in his hands and turning my head from side to side as if inspecting me.

I batted his claw away. "Don't touch me."

Scott released a deep, throaty chuckle. "Lilly Blu was right – you do look like the statue."

"Lilly Blu?" I breathed.

"I told you we couldn't trust the lying bitch-wolf," Potter said.

"Wolf," Scott said, turning on his heels to look at Potter. "Don't you have one living inside of you? Doesn't that make you a wolf, too, Potter?" Without waiting for any reply from Potter, Scott turned his attention back to me. "I understand that you've got some wolf in you, too, Kiera Hudson. Would you like some more?" He grinned, running the length of his jagged claw slowly over my bottom lip and down the length of my neck. He glanced down at my breasts then back up at me, that crooked smile of his never fading.

"Keep your filthy claws off her," Potter said, flying forward. But before he got within reach of me, he was set upon by several wolves that were yapping and snarling nearby.

I shot to his aid, but was held back by Scott. I kicked out at him, but was soon overwhelmed by the other wolves. I raked at them with my claws and gnashed at them with my fangs, but there was too many for me. There were too many for Potter, too, and both of us soon succumbed to them. Pinned flat against the ground, I felt a metal collar being fastened about my throat. I clawed at it, but it was secured tight. A long wrought iron chain was attached to it. One of the wolves pulled on the chain. I made a choking sound in the back of my throat and gagged. The wolf that was yanking on the chain laughed as he dragged me forward along the ground. In fear that I would either be strangled or my neck broken, I scrambled up onto my knees, then my feet. With my eyes watering and gasping for breath, I searched desperately for Potter. At first I couldn't seem him and I felt overwhelmed with panic. With the metal collar about my neck it was hard to see in any other direction than the one the wolf dragged me in. I threw my hands to the collar and tried to wedge them between it and my throat. I was desperate to make myself some breathing space. I felt like I was going to suffocate. I sucked air into my lungs via my nose. I twisted around at the waist, again desperate to lay eyes on Potter. I needed to know that he was safe. But my eyes fell not on Potter but the young girl. Like me, she now wore a thick metal collar about her throat and was being dragged forward through the forest by one of the many wolves who walked upright. I watched her tumble and fall to her knees. She made a rasping sound, throwing her hands to the collar as she made a wheezing noise in the back of her throat. Her frail-looking wings beat on either side of her, the membrane looking almost translucent. Using her wings to help her, she fluttered back to her feet. Seeing this, the wolf leading her like an animal yanked sharply on the chain, dragging her back to the ground again. The wolf howled with delight, its eyes blazing almost red.

"I promise that every one of you fuckers will die for this," I heard Potter say.

I couldn't see him, but his voice was close – somewhere behind me. My heart leapt, knowing that he was still alive.

"And the first to die is gonna be that two-faced bitch, Lilly Blu – ghost or not," Potter continued to rant, his voice sounding breathless and wheezing like he was about to choke. But this didn't stop him. "I'm glad Murphy cut the bitch's head off…. I would've cut her fucking tongue out, too…"

I heard a cracking sound, followed by Potter crying out in pain. He didn't make any more threats after that. The only way I could be sure that he was still alive was the sound of his breathless wheezing he made in the back of his throat as he was dragged – like me and the girl – through the forest, the Lycanthropes' prisoners. But who was the girl? Was she one of the Lycanthropes' prisoners who had escaped? Did they have other Vampyrus imprisoned deep in the forest? Was that the real reason Murphy hated the wolves in this layer? The Potter from this *where* and *when* said that there had been an uneasy truce between the Vampyrus and Lycanthrope but that had ended the moment Murphy had decapitated Lilly Blu. Were we now being punished for Murphy's crime? But I suspected that there was more to our capture than sheer retribution for what Murphy had done. It appeared that Bruce Scott had been expecting me and Potter to arrive. He knew that we both had wolves lurking inside of us. The only person to have known that would've been Lilly Blu, wouldn't it? It would only have been her who knew about Potter and the wolf because it was she who had helped put it there. But I knew that Scott had been expecting me. I could remember the conversation I'd overheard between the two wolves that had beaten Nev to death. They had kidnapped him because they believed he had known something about the statue in Snake Weed – the statue that Scott said looked like me. The wolves who had taken Nev were meant to have taken him back to Scott for interrogation, but they had killed him and I had killed them before they had a chance to do so. Was this what we had been captured for? Was the real reason Scott knew about me and Potter because we had slaughtered those wolves in the valley? But that hadn't been my Potter – that had been the other. And why had Lilly Blu decided to lead us to Scott now and not on the night Potter and I had killed those wolves? Why had she instead led me to the shack with Potter's dead body? Why bring Potter back to me if only to kill us both? None of it made sense. And where was the White Wolf now? Had it deserted us now that it had delivered us to Scott and the other Lycanthrope? Was its work done and would we ever see it again? I didn't have any answers to my questions.

 I was literally dragged from my thoughts by the wolf that continued to yank on the chain about my neck. Stumbling forward, I put my hands out before me to break my fall. I hit the ground hard, causing my knees to make an audible cracking sound. I glanced to my right and could see the girl standing a few feet away. Her head was down, her chin against her chest. She looked tired and beaten. The wolf leading her through the forest tugged violently on her chain as if to wake her from her malaise. Like an obedient animal, the girl raised her head.

"Get up! Get up!!" my personal captor roared at me. The wolf pulled on the chain with its meaty claws. My neck felt as if it was going to snap. I struggled to get to my feet. Looking to my left I saw Potter. He looked bloody and beaten. Blood covered his chin and had dribbled onto his chest. I couldn't be sure how much of the blood belonged to the wolves he had killed or how much was his own. His hair hung in a dark messy flop over his brow as he stood, head bowed forward. I had lost all track of time and I had no idea how long we had been led through the forest by the wolves. I looked up, searching for the faintest glint of sunlight through the canopy of leaves and branches overhead, and stifled a wheezy gasp in the back of my throat. The sky was still dark and the stars were still racing across it at speed, but it wasn't that which had taken my breath away, it was the building that the wolves had led us to.

In the centre of the vast forest stood an ancient building which looked like something close to the Colosseum in Rome. It was made of grey and white stone, and although it was circular in design, it was so vast that it stretched away in both directions for as far as I could see. It loomed over us, fires burning in the giant glassless windows that helped form the colossal structure. One side of the colosseum-type building looked like it had fallen away. Whether it had crumbled down with age or through battle, I didn't know. And although the building was vast and intimidating, it looked beautiful too.

"Welcome to our home," Bruce Scott suddenly said, his voice full of awe as if he too was struck by its beauty every time he looked upon it.

Without saying anything more, Scott strode out toward

the building. The wolf yanked on my chain again and I trotted to keep up. The pain in my throat felt less if the chain that the wolf held was slack and not taut. To be led like an animal toward a building of such grandeur and beauty felt more demeaning than it had done before. I felt like nothing more than an insignificant speck as I was yanked and pulled toward the colosseum-like building as if I was some captured animal. As we were dragged closer and closer to the ancient building, I heard a sound that, at first, I thought could only have been thunder. But I had never heard the roar of thunder sound so loud and terrifying. It was the howl of a thousand or more wolves I could hear coming from inside the colosseum. I glanced at Potter. He raised his head to look at me. The girl to my left began to scream. And for the first time since being *pushed* into this *where* and *when*, I suddenly felt like screaming too.

Chapter Twenty-Four

Kiera

The wolves led us through a goliath-sized gate that was set into the stone wall of the colosseum-like building. The door was so huge that it was pulled open by a series of cranks, pulleys, and levers which were worked by wolves on the other side of it. The iron door that we were being led through screamed on its many hinges and the sound of the howling wolves that I could hear coming from inside the colossal building faded – just a little. Potter, the girl, and I were dragged through the gate and into a dome-shaped passageway. I glanced at Potter and he looked back at me. His eyes were almost puffed shut and swollen with black and purple bruises from where he had been beaten on our journey through the forest. His bottom lip bled onto his chin. Our eyes met only briefly before the chains about our throats were pulled on and again we lurched forward. The girl continued to sob as she was led forward behind me. As we were dragged nearer to the end of the dome-shaped passage I could just see past the hulking figure of Bruce Scott who led the party of wolves. And what I saw turned my stomach to mush. My heart thumped so fast that it felt as if it was being dragged up my throat and into my mouth.

At the end of the passageway, each of us were dragged into a vast amphitheatre. It was like a giant open-air football stadium. And as we were led into its centre, we were utterly dwarfed by its sheer size as it towered high above us on all sides. There was tiered seating on all sides. The rows and rows of seats had been carved out of the stone walls that formed the oval shaped structure. Each seat was occupied by a Lycanthrope. They howled and roared. Stomping their feet so loud that it sounded as if the amphitheatre was rumbling with thunder. I knew very little of ancient Roman history but I knew enough to know that such places had been used for events like gladiator combats, chariot racing, animal slayings, and human executions. As the wolves yanked and pulled us into its centre, the thousands and thousands of Lycanthrope that occupied the seats roared with a rabid excitement. I glanced up at them. Some of the wolves looked just like giant hounds that roamed the inner walls of the amphitheatre, but others looked more like werewolves – trapped somewhere between wolf and human. The ground was covered in sand, dirt, and dust. I looked up at the sky which was still black. The stars continued to race across it at speed and the moon looked little more than a blur as it spun around and around. But there was something else. At first I couldn't be sure what it was I was looking at. From the pit of the amphitheatre, as I looked up at the night sky, it appeared that some giant and intricate web crisscrossed back and forth above the open-air stadium. But it seemed to be moving – or parts of it did. Screwing up my eyes, I craned my neck back as far as I could against the metal collar so I could get a better look at what it was that at first glance appeared to be some elaborate spider's web. A gasp rattled in the back of my throat as I realised that it wasn't a web at all but a complex maze of what looked like a model railway track. Hundreds – no thousands – of what looked like toy trains travelled around and around, back and forth, up and down over the maze of track that crisscrossed the night sky above the amphitheatre. And perhaps what I had first thought to be stars racing across the sky hadn't been so at all, but the tiny headlamps of the trains and the twinkling lights that lit the thousands and thousands of carriages.

As I stood and stared wide-eyed and open-mouthed at the unbelievable spectacle above my head, I could see that some parts of the tracks were sliding back and forth. It was like many invisible hands were pulling and pushing levers somewhere to change the direction of the trains that travelled along the tracks above the amphitheatre. To watch the track continuously shift and change shape – to watch those model trains switch rails and take different paths – was mesmerizing. Running parallel to these tracks were what looked like tiny railway stations, signal boxes, sidings with buffers where some trains had come to the end of their journey. Some stations looked grander than others – some looked little more than remote ticket offices. There was so much to look at – so much to see and with the track layout continuously changing shape and direction I could have watched the hypnotic spectacle forevermore without getting bored.

"What the fuck?" I heard Potter croak beside me.

"I know, it's incredible," I wheezed against my collar. But Potter wasn't looking up at the intricate maze of railway track above our heads – he was looking aghast at something else altogether. I followed his stare and my stomach somersaulted with horror and revulsion. Near to where we were being dragged and pulled across the amphitheatre were a line of male and female Vampyrus. They looked emaciated. They were so thin that I could see their hipbones, ribs, knees, and elbows poking through their paper white skin. Much of their hair had fallen out, either through malnourishment or despair. Their wings were tatty and threadbare. Each of these Vampyrus wore a collar about their neck which was attached to a chain fixed to the floor of the amphitheatre. A dagger whizzed past my line of sight and I followed its path as it thudded into the chest of one of the Vampyrus that had been chained up. Blood jetted from the wound and splashed the dusty ground black. The Vampyrus cried out before dropping face first to the ground, inadvertently driving the blade deeper into his heart. The Vampyrus lay dead on the floor of the amphitheatre, his wings fluttering momentarily before falling limp and still. This side of the colosseum exploded with a roar of delight from the wolves that were packed into tight rows in the tiered seating. Another knife glinted like a streak of lightning as it whisked past just inches from me. I looked to see who had thrown it. There were several wolves, each of them clutching knives in their fists. They were using the chained-up Vampyrus as target practice. They were killing them for sport. Each of them took aim and threw their knives at the weak and frail looking Vampyrus that stood in a line just feet away. One of the wolves threw another of the knives. The female Vampyrus it was intended for furiously beat her wings, rising up from off the ground. But because of the chain fastened about her neck she couldn't fly away – she couldn't escape. The knife shot just beneath her feet as she hovered above the ground, her eyes bright with terror. The wolves in the crowds howled and roared with delight. It happened so fast that I barely saw the glint of the dagger that buried itself squarely into the centre of her face. Her head peeled away to the left and right of the blade in a gush of blood as her face fell apart. She dropped lifeless out of the air and thudded into the ground, sending up a plume of dust. The wolves who were watching the sickening display shot to their feet, punching the air with their claws as they howled with delight.

    I couldn't bear to watch, so I looked away. But in every direction there appeared to be some untold horror taking place. Some wolves had set up a makeshift football pitch in the heart of the amphitheatre. They had erected the corpses of four Vampyrus as goal posts, and for a ball they kicked about a decapitated head. The wolves waiting wailed with a morbid delight. I looked away in revulsion, only for eyes to fall upon another horrific display. A

Vampyrus male had been strung up. Something similar to a chessboard had been tattooed over his upper torso. The game was being played by two wolves who – as they moved the pieces of the game – hammered them in place into the Vampyrus' chest with vicious-looking spikes. When they moved the pieces of the game once more, they ripped them out of the board made of flesh and hammered them into a new position. The male Vampyrus screamed in pain as the wolves took their turn. I covered my ears and shut my eyes. I couldn't bear to watch – I couldn't bear to hear the man's screams. With my eyes closed and the wolf that led me across the vast amphitheatre pulling roughly on my chain, I tripped and stumbled face first into the dirt. The crowd roared once more. I felt the skin peel from the palms of my hands against the coarse ground and I cried out. Tears stung in my eyes, but it wasn't the pain that had put them there but the sights I had seen – the sight of those terrible games the Lycanthrope were making the Vampyrus play. I had never seen anything so macabre and barbaric in my life. Those sights would haunt me for the rest of my life – however long that now might be.

But I had to get out of this nightmare. Both Potter and I had to. If we didn't, then how would what Jack told me ever come true? How would Potter and I ever get married, have a daughter, name her Cara Hudson? How would I ever tell her the story behind the ring that Potter had given to me? Clutching onto those thoughts – *dreams* – with both hands, I struggled back to my feet. I felt a hand close around my arm, as if to help me up. I glanced to my right to discover that it was Potter.

"I love you..." he whispered, before one of the wolves leapt up and crunched his fist into Potter's face. His head rocked back against the collar and a clot of black blood exploded from his mouth. He dropped to his knees, head hung forward. The wolf that led him stepped up and buried his boot into Potter's side. He rolled over into the dirt, his wings now covered with dust.

"Get up!" the wolf demanded, the long hair hanging from his face whipping back and forth, jagged teeth, yellow-stained and broken.

When Potter didn't spring to his feet at once, the wolf said, "Your choice, Potter." He then dragged him forward over the ground and through the dirt and dust by the chain fastened about his neck. I saw Potter's face turn a shade of blue then a dark purple.

"Stop!" I begged. "You're going to kill him."

My pleas went unanswered as the wolf leading me yanked on the chain and I shot forward once more.

Bruce Scott led us to the furthest wall of the amphitheatre. Set into it was another door. This one was made of iron and wasn't as tall or wide as the other that we had first been dragged through. In fact, Scott had to stoop forward to pass through it. We were shoved and pushed into a narrow passageway that was lined on each side with cells. I could hear Potter's body being dragged and pulled along behind me. I wanted to look back to see if he was still alive, but the collar fixed tight about my throat prevented me from doing so. The girl who had been captured along with us staggered forward just feet ahead of me. Gritting my teeth through the pain, I twisted my head to the right as much as I could bear. I peered into the cells that had been hollowed out into the stone walls. In each of them I could see more of those skeletal-looking Vampyruses. The cells were small and narrow and made to look even more claustrophobic than they actually were by the sheer number of prisoners they were home to. Each cell was frighteningly overcrowded. Some of the Vampyrus lay half dead and were stripped bare on the floor, their wings wrapped about them to keep them warm and offer them some last remaining shred of modesty. Others stood propped against the cell doors, their faces gaunt and haunted. They reached weakly through the bars, their brittle fingers clutching and pulling at me.

"Help us," one frail woman begged.

"Please," whimpered another.

"I'm sorry," I whispered, tears burning in my eyes.

Just ahead, I heard the sound of a cell door being thrown open. It rattled and clanked in its frame. In the torch-lit passageway I could see Bruce Scott standing by an open cell door. He pushed the girl in first and I heard her cry out as she hit the floor. Reaching the door, Bruce Scott gripped me by the shoulders.

"Why?" I asked him.

Without saying anything, he forced me into the cell. I fell to my knees, the chain clanking about my neck. Potter was dragged in behind me, his battered and lifeless-looking body scraping over the filthy floor of the cell. The girl crawled to the furthest corner of the cell, drawing her knees up to her chest. The wolves left and I glanced up to see Scott close the door. He looked at me through the bars before turning away and heading back down the passageway.

Crawling forward on my hands and knees, I pulled Potter up into my arms and cradled him to my chest.

"I hope you can *see* a way out of this..." he whispered, before falling into unconsciousness.

Chapter Twenty-Five

Kiera

"What did he say?"

The voice was soft – nothing more than a whisper really, and at first I wondered if I hadn't imagined it. The sounds of the wolves' howling and barking in the amphitheatre was still so loud that it was hard to hear myself think, let alone anything else. The excited calls almost seemed to come in thunderous waves as they washed down into the passageway and the cells. There was no window in the cell and the only light came from a torch that flickered in a bracket fixed into the wall. The collar still felt stiff about my neck, but now that I didn't have a wolf dragging me along by it, I felt as if I could at least breathe more easily.

"What did he say?" the voice came again, this time slightly louder.

With Potter resting in my lap, I looked up and across the cell. It was the young girl who had spoken. She was peering at me over the top of her knees which she had drawn up and tucked beneath her chin. She sat against the far side of the cell, almost completely hidden in the shadows. She stared at me with her dark round eyes. Her long black hair lay straight about her face, which I could now see was very pretty despite being pale and drawn. Perhaps she was slightly older than the fifteen years I had first believed her to be. With so much grime and dirt plastered to her face, it was hard to tell.

"What is this place?" I asked, keeping my voice low so as not to scare her again.

"It's a prison," she said. "It's where the wolves bring us – the Vampyrus. They play games with us – they torture us – but mostly they just kill us."

"But why?" I asked.

"Because they hate us, I guess," she said with a faint shrug of her bony shoulders.

Gently wiping blood from around Potter's mouth with my fingertips, I looked back at the girl and said, "What were you doing in the forest?"

"I'd escaped," she said, her eyes not leaving me, that haunted expression still drawn down over her face.

"Escaped? How did you manage to escape from a place like this?" I asked. To hear her say such a thing sparked hope in me. If such a delicate looking girl as her could find a way out, then perhaps I could too.

"Some of the guards like me to dance for them – I like dancing," she said. "There was one guard in particular who liked me – you know – in a way that perhaps he shouldn't have. He wasn't as nasty to me as some of the others. So I pretended that I liked him back too…" the young girl trailed off, staring right through me – like she was seeing something that only she could.

"You don't have to tell me," I said softly. "I don't want you to talk about something that you would rather forget or that makes you feel…"

"No, it's okay," she whispered, refocusing on me. "I let the guard get close to me – I let him believe that perhaps I liked him the same way that he liked me. He would have been in trouble if he'd been found out. Mixing between Lycanthrope and Vampyrus is forbidden. It can create abominations – half and halfs. Creatures that are half wolf and half Vampyrus. Have you ever heard of such a thing?"

I nodded my head slowly. "I seem to remember hearing

something like that."

"Well, this wolf was thinking too much about what he'd like to do with me rather than guarding me," the girl said. "I told him that I would only – only mix with him if he unchained me. After sitting and watching me dance for him, conjuring all sorts of vile images in his head of what might happen next, he unchained me. It was at that moment I struck. I flew away, over the walls but not before I clawed the filthy wolf's eyes out," she said, glancing down at her hands. That's why the wolves were chasing me – hunting for me. I thought you were part of them when you came after me. I didn't realise that you were Vampyrus too. I'm sorry if I hurt you or your friend."

"You didn't hurt us," I said. "I'm sorry if we scared you – I'm sorry if we played some part in your recapture"

Potter made a groaning sound as he flinched restlessly in my lap. Was he fighting with the wolf again? Had the wolf come forward inside of him? The wolf inside me had remained ominously silent since our capture by the wolves.

"Is he going to be okay?" the girl asked, still cradling herself in the corner.

"I hope so," I said, looking down into his face and gently brushing hair from his brow.

"You never answered my question?" the girl said.

I glanced up at her. "Huh? What question was that?"

"What did he say before he fell unconscious?"

"He asked whether I could see a way out of here," I said.

"Do you *see* stuff then?" the girl asked, still peering at me over the top of her knees.

"Sometimes," I said.

"What like?"

"I don't know," I shrugged. "It's hard to explain."

"Do you *see* people – like people that are dead?"

I frowned at her. "I'm not sure I know what you mean?"

"I used to *see* this dead guy," the girl said, her voice dropping to a whisper as if fearing that she might be overheard. "He used to show me stuff."

"What kind of stuff?" I asked, my interest suddenly intensifying.

"Murders and stuff like that. He would show me where the dead bodies were – the bodies of those murdered by the wolves. That's why I'm here. They say that I was the one who really killed the wolves that I found or how else would I have known where the dead bodies were hidden. But I think they were scared that I would be able to identify the killer – it was like they didn't want to know – didn't want to believe – there was a killer of wolves amongst them."

"Did you ever learn who this killer was?" I asked.

"I don't remember," the girl said.

I pulled a face of disbelief at her. "You don't remember? What kind of answer is that?"

"The wolves made me not remember," the girl said. "I can't even remember my own name. Where I come from – who I am."

"How did they make you forget?" I asked.

She dropped her voice again to a whisper. "They operated on me – did tests on me."

"What kind of tests?"

Without saying anything, the girl drew back her long black hair from the side of her face. In the gloom, all I could see was a patch of her hair that had been shaved away above her right ear in a crescent shape. Wanting to get a better look at what she was trying to show me, I eased Potter from my lap, placing him down on the floor.

"Fucking wolves," he cursed under his breath, eyelids

flickering before falling still again.

Leaving Potter to rest and to his nightmares, I made my way across the cell, dragging the weighty chain behind me. I knelt beside the girl. She didn't flinch away like she had before. I looked at the shaved patch of skin. I put a hand to my mouth to stifle the gasp that threatened there. I looked at the red garish wounds that marked her flesh behind her ear and along the side of her head. Each wound was circular and about the size of a penny.

"They drilled holes into my skull," the girl said, letting her hair fall back into place and hiding the wounds again.

"Who did?" I said, fearing what other horrors I might be confronted with in this place of hell that I now found myself in.

"The wolves did," she said. "One of them claims to be a doctor of sorts, but I'm not so sure. Her name is Doctor Lane."

Feeling utterly bewildered and confused as to why anyone would want to commit such acts of torture on the young girl, I said, "Why did she do it? Why make holes in your skull?"

"She said she was going to let the voices out – release the young man that I said I could see – the one who told me where to find the dead bodies that the killer – the wolf – had left behind." The girl stared at me with her black eyes. They had that vacant look again, like she was staring at something that only she could see. "Perhaps Doctor Lane was right," the girl suddenly whispered. "I don't see my friend anymore. I don't hear his voice either."

"What was his name?" I asked.

"Martin, I think," she said with a frown as if struggling to remember. "Yes, that was it. His name was Martin and he showed me all kinds of stuff. He let me *see* things that nobody else could."

"Tell me about him," I whispered. "Tell me what this Doctor Lane did to you."

"She was always asking questions and it didn't matter how

often I answered them, it was never good enough. It was never the answer that she wanted to hear. Doctor Lane would ask dumb questions like...

Chapter Twenty-Six

Girl

"How did you know where the body was hidden?" Doctor Lane asked me.

"You know the answer to that," I said back, just wanting to get up and leave. But of course I couldn't – the straps fixed tight about my wrists and ankles made sure of that.

"Tell me again," Doctor Lane smiled in that patronising way I had come to dislike since being sent to the prison.

I glanced to my right, at Martin who sat there, the suit that he wore was tired looking, frayed around the edges, and spattered with mud. His suit was ancient looking, like something someone would have worn many years ago, perhaps a hundred years ago – from the late 1800's. Martin wore a watch on a chain that hung from his waistcoat. He sat forward in the chair so the wings that sprouted from his back didn't get crushed behind him. His hands rested on his knees, a cigarette dangling from his fingers, the other clutching a cloth cap. He shot a glance back at me, winked, then offered me a half smile. Martin had a lovely smile.

"Answer the question," Doctor Lane snapped at me again as I lay strapped to the bed in the makeshift operating theatre beneath the colosseum.

"Huh?" I looked back at her. She wore a white lab coat that was covered with blood spatters. She looked more like a butcher than a real doctor.

"You look distracted again," she smiled. But the smile

wasn't genuine. I could see that. Her face was wolf-like – yet still bore some human traits. Her hands were long and slender, the fingernails sharpened into what looked like points.

"How did your father's death make you feel?' she jumped in, keen to eke out any opportunity of getting me to open up to her. Perhaps find a mistake or an untruth in my story – to get me to confess to all those murders.

"I thought you'd imprisoned me here to talk about the body?" I stared at her from the operating table.

She did that crooked smiling thing again with her mouth so that I could see the points of her teeth, and said, "We can talk about anything you want to. I'm here to help you, not hurt you."

I glanced right again at Martin. He rolled his eyes at me, sucked on the end of the cigarette that now dangled from the corner of his mouth, and blew smoke into the air. I watched it drift in a blue haze toward Doctor Lane, but she seemed not to be bothered by it.

"Do you want to talk about how you knew where that body was?" she pushed.

"What's the point?" I asked. "I mean, I've been dragged from my cell every day for the last three months and I've told you over and over again how I knew where the body was. I haven't done anything wrong. I never killed any wolf. I just want to be set free. I just want to go home."

With her smile fading she said, "You know that's not going to happen. Or…"

"Or what?" I asked, my hands and feet turning numb from where the straps had been fixed too tight.

"Perhaps if you confessed – admitted that it was really you who has been murdering wolves, I could speak on your behalf to Scott…"

"But I'm not the killer," I insisted. "I didn't kill anyone."

Doctor Lane peered over the top of her glasses at me. Why did she wear them? Weren't wolves meant to have perfect eyesight? Did she wear them to make her look more like a real doctor – like she could be trusted and that she wasn't going to hurt me? I guessed she was in her mid-fifties, which was still young for a female wolf – but the glasses made her look more like sixty – and that wasn't so young. Maybe she wore them to hide something. Martin would show me if she had stuff that she wanted to hide.

"Are you evil or just mad?" she asked me, her eyes fixed on mine.

"Neither," I said back.

I saw the edges of her mouth tighten with frustration. "Do I really need to explain the seriousness of the situation you are in? You've been sent to this prison because you're a killer... you're just a teenage girl..."

"I'm not a killer," I reminded her and out of the corner of my eye I saw my friend Martin offer me another boyish grin.

Peering at me over the rim of her glasses again, she added, "So how did you know where the body was hidden?"

I shot a glance at Martin, who was now picking at the mud from his suit with his dirty fingernails and flicking it onto Lane's clean operating theatre floor. He looked at me and shrugged as if he didn't know how to convince the doctor either that I was telling the truth. I cocked an eyebrow at him as if to say, *help me out here, can't you?*

He just grinned back at me and said, "You're on your own, girl." I hated the way he always called me "girl." It wasn't as if he was much older than me, he was twenty-four. But he was always so bloody cocky about everything.

"Only you know the answer," Doctor Lane said, and I looked back at her.

"I *see* things," I told her and not for the first time. I had been trying to tell her this for the last few months – but I was yet to convince her.

"How so? What do you mean exactly – you *see* things?"

"You know what I mean," I said. "Look, Doctor Lane, I don't wish to be rude, but we've been over and over this. I've told you what happened. Do I really need to tell you again?"

"Humour me," she smiled, flashing her jagged teeth.

"I'm not here to entertain you, Doctor Lane," I said, yanking on the restraints. I'd rather be back in my cell than have to put up with her. "Why must we keep having to go over and over the same stuff? I'm not going to ever change my story. I'm not going to admit to killing those wolves – I'm not going to admit to something I haven't done."

"Tell the doctor what you saw," Martin suddenly spoke up.

"But I've gone over it so many times before," I said, turning my head to look at him. He continued to sit in the chair, wearing his shabby suit, muddy boots, and sporting an unshaven chin.

"Go on, tell her," he said. "Then we can get out of here."

Did Martin really believe that? Did he really think that Doctor Lane or Bruce Scott would ever let me go?

"Talk to me," Lane said again, the sudden kindness in her voice making her sound patronising and fake.

I turned my head away from Martin. But this time, I couldn't bring myself to look into Doctor Lane's eyes. I had seen enough already.

"Tell me what you saw?" she hushed, like a mother trying to coax the truth from a naughty child. "Tell me how you knew where to find the dead body of the wolf."

"You want me to tell you how I knew where the body of that young female wolf was hidden? You want me to tell you how

I knew the killer was six foot tall, that he enjoyed hill walking, how that victim had fought with him? That he had recently visited the place where he was going to kill her and that it was nearby to where she had been taken. You want me to tell you how I knew that she was already dead, even though it had only been an hour since her disappearance? You want me to tell you how I knew where that place was going to be?"

"I'd love you to tell me," Doctor Lane almost seemed to beam.

I glanced at Martin again. Then, pointing at him, I said, "He showed me."

Doctor Lane looked in the direction that I was pointing. Martin waved at her. Turning to face me with that smile again, Lane said, "We've been over this before. There is no one sitting in that chair."

"Who's that in the picture?" I asked Doctor Lane.

She looked away from the chair where Martin sat and back at the picture which hung from the wall above a metal table that was home to an array of sharply pointed instruments. The picture was of two young Lycanthrope girls – identical twins by the look of them. Lane faced me again, trying to keep her face expressionless – but she couldn't hide the pain I could see in her eyes.

"We're not here to discuss my family photos," she said stiffly.

"Oh, I'm sorry, it's just that…" I started but she didn't let me finish.

"So is Martin – this Vampyrus friend of yours here right now?"

"Yes," I told her and glanced at him. Martin smiled, his face wan, but his eyes sparkled as if he was going to enjoy what was coming. We had been here before. He knocked aside the flop of black hair that fell across his brow.

"I can't see him," Doctor Lane told me, a smile making the corners of her mouth twitch.

"You never can," I reminded her, and looked across at him.

"I'm over here!" he shouted at Lane, waving his arms above his head at her. "I'm sitting right here, sweetheart!" He sat forward in his seat again, wings thrumming behind him.

I looked back at Lane and she was staring blankly at the chair. "There is no one there. I suggest you take another look."

"I don't need to. He's there," I insisted.

Doctor Lane crossed the makeshift operating theatre and stood in front of the chair that Martin occupied. He looked up at her, a wide smile stretched across his rugged face.

"She's going to sit on my lap again, isn't she?" he asked, glancing at me.

"You know it," I said, trying to stifle a giggle by placing my fingertips to my lips.

And we were right. No sooner had I spoken, then Doctor Lane had dropped herself into the chair. But, Martin was quick – I mean he was real quick when he wanted to be. I didn't know if it came with being dead – but sometimes he moved so fast that he was nothing more than a blur.

Doctor Lane, with a look of satisfaction blazing across her face, said, "See, there is no one here. The chair is empty. Where is this Martin now?'

He was standing right in front of her. He stood, shoulders rolled back, wings humming loudly. Couldn't she hear them? His suit looked heavy on his wiry frame, the material made of thick uncomfortable-looking cloth.

"So where is he?" Doctor Lane asked again, peering at me over the rim of her glasses.

"Doctor Lane! Doctor Lane! I'm right here!" Martin

shouted, waving his hands right in front of her face. He looked back at me and winked.

"Stop it!" I told him.

"Stop what?" Lane smiled. "I'm only trying to help you."

"I wasn't talking to you" I said.

Leaning back in the chair, Doctor Lane folded her arms across her chest and said, "No, I won't stop. By me reinforcing this delusion – this *fantasy* – of yours, isn't going to help you. You need to admit that it was you who murdered that young female wolf."

"You'll never convince her," Martin said, looking at me. "You know she's going to need some proof if she's ever going to believe you." Then, walking behind her, he gently placed his hands on her shoulders. I looked at Lane and she was totally unaware that he was touching her. She just stared across the room at me, waiting for me to say something. But I was too busy looking at Martin with a morbid curiosity because I knew what he was about to do and what would happen next.

Taking Doctor Lane by the shoulders, Martin rolled his head back and started to hum. He always hummed the same song – It was that hymn - *The Lord of the Dance* – the one about dancing with the devil on your back. I didn't know why it was always that particular tune.

"Why do you always hum that?" I had asked him once.

"Why not?" he'd winked back. "I just like it – it helps me."

The torches that were along the walls of the operating room flickered as Martin started to hum. It wasn't rushed, just slow, a pause between notes as if he was somehow savouring the moment. Then the smell came. It was weak at first, but with every second that passed it grew stronger, and as Lane sat staring at me, totally unaware of what was going to happen, I discreetly took a deep breath. She would never smell it, but I would. At its worst, it made me want to gag.

It was the smell of decay – rotting flesh. Flesh which had putrefied over many years, gone sloppy and run from the bones that it had once covered. As I sat and listened to Martin hum, he held Doctor Lane by the shoulders, and that smell seeped from him like a mist – an invisible vapour.

Then, rolling his head forward again, he stared ahead, as if concentrating on something that only he could see. But he didn't look like Martin anymore and this was the part that I hated the most. I dreaded each time it happened. To see him made my stomach knot as if my own intestines had been reduced to slop. Gone were his blue eyes, the nose that looked as if it had been broken too many times, the cleft chin, and his mop of thick black hair. His face was decayed and raw looking. His eyes were now black, and rolled back into two sunken sockets that appeared to bore right back into his skull. The flesh that covered his face was paper thin, and had a translucent look to it. And as he hummed, I could see his jawbones clenching through his skin. Most of his hair had fallen away, and what was left stood out in black clumps. His suit hung from his emaciated frame.

To see him in this decayed state scared me – but not how you would think. Martin didn't scare me – I scared myself because to look at him made me realise that I too would look just like that one day. I pushed those fears from my mind and looked at Martin as his dead black eyes stared straight ahead, over the top of Doctor Lane's head and at the picture of the twin wolves on her desk.

Martin stopped humming and said, "One of them is dead. In water. Not too deep. Shallow. But she didn't drown. No, not that. I don't want to see that. Move slightly. Go on – that's right. There's a good girl."

And as he muttered and mumbled to himself, I looked at

Doctor Lane sitting in the chair, arms folded across her chest.

"Well?" she said.

"Well what?" I asked, having totally lost the thread of the conversation we'd been having.

"Have I convinced you yet that you don't have a friend called Martin?" she pushed. "A friend that is dead and who shows you where to find..."

"He's dead, all right," I breathed, glancing up at him as he stood and mumbled away to himself.

"So you finally agree that even if you did once have a friend called Martin, he couldn't possibly be in this room with us and that he couldn't have possibly helped you find that dead girl because he's dead himself?"

I stole another deep breath as the stench that seeped from Martin's rotting corpse became almost suffocating. I could feel tears standing in my eyes as they started to water.

"Don't upset yourself," Doctor Lane said, her voice softening, believing my tears were through sadness.

"Hey," Martin whispered in my direction but not taking his eyes from the picture of the two wolves. "This is so sad."

"Please stop," I asked him, my voice barely a whisper, just like his own.

"I'm almost beginning to feel sorry for Doctor Lane," he said, his black eyes rolling like crazy in their sunken sockets. And every time he spoke, I could see his tongue moving through his cheek. It reminded me of how my father had made the shadows of animals with his hands against my bedroom wall when I was a child. "You've got to see this," Martin added.

"Stop," I told him again.

"But we can't stop," Doctor Lane said, still believing that it was only her and I in the room. "I need you to admit to being a killer."

"Listen to the Doctor," Martin half smiled, never taking his eyes off the picture of the two young girls on the desk.

"But I'm scared," I told him.

"There is nothing to fear," Lane continued with her psychological bullshit.

"Doctor Lane has a point," Martin smirked and his lips rolled back to reveal a set of grey fleshy gums. Then, he was muttering to himself again as whatever it was he was *seeing* played out before him. I knew that it was only moments before he would show me too. But I didn't want to see stuff about Doctor Lane. I didn't want to know her secrets. It would change the way I felt about her. I was angry with her – I resented her – hated her for strapping me to the table and being one of those who had imprisoned me for crimes that I hadn't committed. For crimes I could help them to solve if only she would believe me. I didn't want to feel sorry for Doctor Lane – I didn't want to feel pity for her."

"You've got to see this," Martin whispered in my direction.

"I don't want to see it," I hissed, yanking my wrist against the restraints that held me down.

"Sooner or later you're going to have to see that by living in this fantasy world that you've created isn't helping you..." Lane started up again.

"I'm not talking to you," I barked, glaring at her through the strands of hair that dangled in front of my face.

"So who are you talking to?" Lane shot back at me.

"You know who I'm freaking talking to," I told her, my heart beginning to quicken.

"Your imaginary friend – accomplice?" she sneered, rolling back her top lip to reveal her pointed teeth.

"His name is Martin," I told her through my hair. "Now can we just stop this? Can't you just let me go?"

"Only you can stop it," Lane said in her patronising tone. And how if I could break free – I would commit murder for the very first time.

"You've really got to see this," Martin said.

"I don't want to," I told him.

"Then I have no choice but to operate," Doctor Lane said, turning to the table where the sharp-looking blades, saws, and a knife were laid out.

"How many ways do I have to tell you this, I'm not talking to you!" I yelled at her, screwing my fists into balls and yanking against my restraints.

"I really don't see any point in continuing with this," Doctor Lane sniffed, picking up something that looked very much like a rusty drill from off the metal table. She turned the wooden handle and the drill bit began to spin around and around like a corkscrew.

"You've upset her now," Martin cut in, as he rolled his head back again and started to hum. He had seen everything there was for him to see and now came the sharing part.

"Piss off," I told him.

"Okay, have it your way," Lane said coming across the operating theatre toward me with the drill in her hand. "Perhaps I need to find a way of releasing that voice – Martin's voice – that seems to be haunting you so much."

Martin stopped humming. He rolled his head forward again and looked at me with his blue eyes. Gone was the decay, the sunken eye sockets, and see-through flesh.

"Do you want to *see*?" he asked me.

I shook my head knowing that it would only be a matter of time before he gripped my hand in his and showed me what he had seen. And just like I knew he would, Martin came and stood beside the operating table and entwined his fingers with mine. His long dark wings trailed behind him. My head rocked back against the operating table and my whole body went stiff. I screwed my eyes shut and in the darkness behind my lids, Martin showed me how one of Doctor's Lane's daughters had died. Martin showed me Doctor Lane shoving her daughter's head beneath the water of a vast lake. The water was crimson like blood. There was a fountain and the water was running upwards as if back into heaven. Doctor Lane was crying as she drowned her own daughter. Why had she killed her?

"Stop!" I cried out, not wanting Martin to show me any more.

"Sorry?" Lane asked me.

I opened my eyes and looked up into hers. She had the drill poised above me. "Wait!" I said.

She peered at me over her glasses.

"I'll tell you everything," I whispered.

"Everything?"

"This should be interesting," Martin said, taking his seat again and lighting another cigarette.

"I'll tell you the truth," I promised. "I'll tell you how I knew where to find that girl. I'll tell you where the murderer has killed before. And I'll tell you his name and where you can find him. But you might not like what else I have to say."

"And what might that be?" she asked, pushing the tip of the drill bit against my skull.

Looking over her shoulder at the picture on the wall, I said, "Because at the end of my story, I'll tell you what happened to one of those two little girls in that photograph and then you'll have to believe me. Everyone will believe me."

Not looking back at the picture, Doctor Lane fixed me with her bright eyes. "When I've finished with you, you won't remember a thing... not even your name," she said as she started to bore the first of many holes into my skull and I started to scream.

Chapter Twenty-Seven

Kiera

"And Doctor Lane was right," the girl said, tears brimming in her eyes as she sat and cradled herself. "I can't remember my name. All I can remember about anything is what I've told you. It's like I don't know anything more than what I've told you."

"And what about your friend, Martin?" I asked, kneeling before her. I gently took one of her hands in mine to offer some crumb of comfort. I didn't know if she really had had a friend only she could *see* – a friend who showed her where to find dead people. Who was I to judge her? "Do you hear him – see him anymore?"

"No," the girl said, shaking her head, tears spilling onto her cheeks. "I have no one."

"You have me," I shrugged.

"I don't even know you," she said.

"I'm Kiera Hudson," I smiled.

Potter made a groaning sound behind me. I looked back to see him roll onto his side. "Fuck you," he grumbled deliriously. "Fuck the wolves."

"And that's Potter," I said, looking back at the girl.

"Are you like married or something?" the girl asked, arming the tears from her cheek. Some of the dirt and grime came away and she looked prettier still.

"We're engaged... just," I said, glancing down at the ring Potter had given to me.

The girl followed my stare and looked at the ring. "That's

real pretty," she said.

"It used to belong to Potter's mother," I told her. "But she's..."

"But what?" the girl asked, combing a length of loose hair behind her ear.

"It doesn't matter," I said. Then changing the subject, I added, "If you can't remember your name, what should I call you?"

"I don't know," the girl said, with a shrug. "I've always thought the name Cara was kind of pretty."

"Really?" I said, slowly sliding my hand from hers.

"But what about a last name – I'll need one of those, don't you think?" the girl said, staring at me.

"I guess," I breathed, my skin suddenly turning tight with gooseflesh.

"I like your surname," the girl said.

"Hang on... there must be another name..." I cut in.

"Hudson. That sounds cool," the girl smiled at me. "From now on, I shall call myself Cara Hudson."

To be continued...

Kiera Hudson & The Origins of Cara

(Kiera Hudson Series Three) Book Six

Kiera Hudson will return soon!

Flip the page to read the first three chapters from the #1 Bestselling series, *'Werewolves of Shade'* By Tim O'Rourke

WEREWOLVES OF SHADE
1

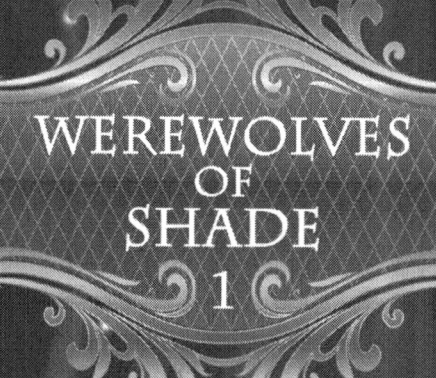

TIM O'ROURKE

Werewolves of Shade

(Beautiful Immortals Series)

Part One

BY

Tim O'Rourke

First Edition Published by Ravenwoodgreys

Copyright 2015 by Tim O'Rourke

This book is a work of fiction. The names, characters, places, and incidents are products of the writer's imagination or have been used fictitiously and are not to be construed as real. Any resemblance to persons, living or dead, actual events, locales or organisations is entirely coincidental.

This eBook is licensed for your personal enjoyment only. This eBook may not be re-sold or given away to other people. If you would like to share this book with another person, please purchase an additional copy for each recipient. If you're reading this book and did not purchase it, or it was not purchased for your use only, then please purchase your own copy. Thank you for respecting the hard work of this author.

Story Editor

Lynda O'Rourke

Book cover designed by:

Tom O'Rourke

Copyedited by:

Carolyn M. Pinard

www.cjpinard.com

For Patrick

Authors note:

The book you hold in your hands or on your favourite e-reading device is the first part of a longer story about the 'Werewolves of Shade'. I've chosen to serialise the story and publish each part in novella length bites. This I have done for a couple of reasons. Chapbooks like this have been around a very long time, in fact Charles Dickens used to publish his stories in this way, not that I am for one minute comparing myself to such a gifted writer. More recent authors have also published works in this way too.

As a kid I used to love watching the old Batman and Flash Gordon episodes on Saturday morning TV. Each episode would end on an agonising cliff-hanger and I would have to wait until the following week to discover how Batman and Robin freed themselves from the shark infested pool they had been dropped into or how Flash would escape the exploding spaceship he was trapped in. And although I found the wait between episodes agonising it was also a lot of fun too as I discussed with my friends on the school yard how our heroes might escape. It set my imagination on fire coming up with my own ideas and theories. Of course I was never right – I never came close - but that didn't matter. It was the fact those stories really came alive in my head – they kept me on the edge of the sofa dying for more. That sense of adventure and excitement has never left me and is one of the reasons I love to write today. I still watch TV shows like *Lost* and *Breaking Bad*, all of them leaving me clawing my eyes out with a strange delight at the cliff-hanger endings!

So within this series, I hope in some small way I help to create that sense of adventure and fun those old TV shows used to create for me. I aim to publish new parts of the story each month until the story is complete (I have three, perhaps four, planned). Each part will end on a cliff-hanger and I hope that you, just like I used to, will come up with your own theories and ideas of how our heroine, Mila Watson, survives the nightmare that will be the 'Werewolves of Shade'.

Best wishes and thanks for reading

Tim O'Rourke

Werewolves of Shade

(Part One)

This story is set in a *where* and *when* not too dissimilar to our own...

Chapter One

All the people of Shade had gone missing. Vanished, some said. Others believed they were all dead, murdered by werewolves. All I knew was that the village of Shade wasn't like any other in England. The country in which I lived had once been very different, but that had been many years ago – a long time before I had been born. It was hard for anyone to know what really had happened to my country or the rest of the world. All any of us knew was that the werewolves and vampires had gone to war.

Yes, there had been werewolves and vampires. They had lived in secret amongst the humans, forging out lives for themselves beneath the noses of the people who had occupied the world back then. According to the rumours and myths that now passed amongst the people of England like whispers, the werewolves and vampires had always been at war. This war had raged in secret, without the humans' knowledge. But like all wars, they become contagious – stretching out across the world, touching all lands and countries. From what little I can gather from the few books and newspapers that remain from that time, the werewolves were trying to protect the humans from vampires. If the werewolves were to be believed, the real threat to humanity came from vampires who wanted to feed off the humans. But of course, the vampires said it was the werewolves the humans had to fear, for it was believed that they wanted to steal human children from their beds and occupy their infant souls.

So the war raged between the werewolves and the vampires as the human world was destroyed. What chance did we humans have of winning a war against two armies of supernatural creatures that could change shape at will, run and leap at incredible speeds, and had the strength of ferocious beasts but the beauty of gods and goddesses? And even if the humans had found a way of matching them, the werewolves and vampires had a strength that could never be matched. They didn't die. Myth had it that even though the world was being destroyed by these creatures, the humans named them the *Beautiful Immortals*.

So why didn't these beautiful immortals completely destroy the world, themselves, and the humans? Legend says that someone came who saved us — she saved the world. And so much like the rest of what happened to the world back then, there is very little recorded about this young woman. But I've listened to folk talk about her in hushed tones. Some say she was the most beautiful of the immortals. I've heard people say that her hair was raven black and her skin as pale as snow. But of course this is all just gossip — no one knows for sure. I should know. I came to want to be an investigative reporter because of the stories I grew up listening to about this woman who came and brought an end to the war between the werewolves and the vampires. Some say that she wasn't like the other beautiful immortals — she was different in some way. But could there really have lived such a creature? And if so, where had she come from? Some said that she was a vampire and I've heard stories that she was seen to climb out of the ground — from a grave. Others said that she was a werewolf and wore the skin of others and could change her appearance at will. I kind of like that story, but my favourite was that this young woman had been neither werewolf nor vampire, but a witch. Rumour has it that this young woman bewitched both the werewolves and vampires, turning them to stone statues which over time became nothing but dust. The story had to be made up, just like all the others. And if she had been real, what had been her name? Are people too scared to say it? And why would that be? If the stories I'd grown up listening to were true and this young woman had saved us humans, why wouldn't people speak her name? I had once asked my father this as I'd sat on his lap as a nine-year-old girl, wondering if this nameless woman who had saved the world had ever really existed.

"Of course she existed, Mila," my father had said, pulling me close and wrapping his arms about my shoulders. "All the werewolves and vampires had gone. She turned them all to stone – to statues."

"But how can you be sure?" I'd asked as we sat before the fire.

"Because there is a statue of her too. It is the only statue of the beautiful immortals that still remains. Unlike the other statues, the statue of this woman has never crumbled to dust," he said.

"A statue?" I gasped. "Where is this statue?"

"I'm not sure," my father had said, scratching his head.

"There is no statue," I grumbled, sliding from his lap, the sudden sense of disappointment crushing my heart. "It's all just a big lie."

"What if I find this statue?" my father asked me. "What if I took you to see it? Would you believe then?"

"No young woman came and saved us," I said, looking at him in the firelight.

"Then why did the war come to an end?" my mother suddenly asked from the doorway of the small house we lived in on the outskirts of the town of Maze. She shook rain from her coat, came inside, and warmed herself by the fire. "What happened to the wolves and the vampires?"

I looked at my mother. Her hair was dark brown like mine and hung in wet streaks to the sides of her pale face and onto her shoulders. "Some say that the werewolves and vampires aren't dead at all, but have snuck back to those places they keep secret from the humans," I said.

"Who told you this...?" my mother started.

"It's just stories I've overheard. But it doesn't matter - it's all just a lie. No one really knows what happened to the werewolves and vampires," I insisted, shaking my young head from side to side.

"Then our lives have all been just one big lie," my father said.

"What do you mean?" I frowned.

"You know me and your mother have spent our lives trying to find out more about this young woman," my father started. "That's why we both became investigative journalists, to try and uncover the truth of what happened in the past."

"You work for the town's newspaper – the newspaper owned by your brother. No one outside the town of Maze reads it," I reminded him.

He looked a little hurt by my words, but I hadn't meant to belittle where my mother and father worked.

"Mila Watson," my mother spoke up, placing one hand on her hip. "You show your father some respect."

"I didn't mean to be disrespectful," I said, looking at the both of them. And I truly hadn't meant to be hurtful. I loved both my parents very much but I felt frustrated that they were wasting their time. Even as a nine-year-old girl, the only thing I really did believe in was that my parents were chasing nothing more than shadows and gossip. But it's not easy to be honest with yourself when you're only nine, and now at the age of nineteen, I knew it had been me who had been lying to myself. I was more like my parents than perhaps I'd ever wanted to admit. My hunger for the truth about what had really happened to the werewolves and the vampires was as much as my parents' had been. And like them, I too wanted to know if humans had been saved by a mysterious young woman with flowing black hair and flesh has cold as stone.

But I never did get the chance to tell my parents how very sorry I was for saying what I had to them that night. The following day, the people from the village of Shade went missing – and so did both my parents.

Chapter Two

From the age of nine I was raised by my uncle Sidney. I left the small house that I had once shared with my parents, what few belongings I had folded neatly into a battered leather case and thrown onto the backseat of the beat up old truck he drove. It was so covered with rust that I feared it would disintegrate all around me as we made our way through the town of Maze. The truck wasn't new; it was a relic from the past – from the time of the war between the werewolves and the vampires. The humans who had survived had taken what the war had burnt or destroyed and tried to breathe new life into it. Who Uncle Sidney's truck had once belonged to, I had no idea, I guessed neither did he. He had driven the truck ever since I could remember and I suspected it was something he had once come across on some remote and desolate road that was cracked with age and the scars of war.

I can remember sitting silently upfront next to my uncle as he steered the ancient vehicle over the cobbled streets that snaked their way through town. Looking past my reflection in the dirty window, I peered out at the streets. The town of Maze in which I had been raised had been named as such because of the maze of empty streets that crisscrossed it. Many of the streets were nothing more than broken piles of rubble where haunted-looking children played war games and made camps. There weren't many schools in England, and most children were taught how to read and write by their parents. There were very few books in this new world and very few had survived the war. I'd heard that in the past, words had stopped being written down on paper and had been written on devices called laptops and android phones. Books had been read on these. People in the past had stopped writing letters on paper and instead sent messages by something some say was called Wi-Fi. But whatever Wi-Fi had truly been, it no longer existed. Some parts of England had no power or electricity at all. The town of Maze went through spells of having power, then was suddenly thrown into weeks and sometimes months of darkness. When this happened, and the nights were long, black and cold, the night-watchmen would patrol the cobbled streets carrying lanterns to cast some light into the utter darkness. The night-watchmen, I guessed, were like what the old world would have once called police officers.

"Where are my parents?" I'd asked my uncle as he had lifted me from his rust-infested truck. He planted me down on the ground outside his home.

"I don't know," he'd said, breaking my stare and taking my case from the backseat of his truck. Taking my hand in his, he led me inside his home where he lived alone. As far as I knew, my Uncle Sidney had never married and didn't have any children of his own. My father had said that his brother was somewhat of a recluse and spent most of his time either fixing up the abandoned house he occupied on the other side of town, or worked late into the night on the newspaper he had started to produce in the old shack at the back of the grounds he had claimed as his.

I was soon to learn that my uncle was a man of few words. He wasn't mean to me or anything like that. In fact, he was very kind and looked after me well. It was as if he was troubled in some way. Those first few days living at my uncle's house were confusing ones. I couldn't understand what had happened to my parents. Had they vanished? Been taken? Or worse still, left me because of what I had said to them that night. Had my words hurt them so much that they no longer wanted to be near me? Is that why, every time I asked my Uncle Sidney where my parents were and when they would come back, he would shrug his broad shoulders and look away. Could he not find the courage in his heart to tell me that my parents had abandoned me?

So in the dim glow of candlelight, I would sit in the corner of the shack and watch my uncle crank the handle of the ancient-looking printer that he used to produce the newspaper for the townsfolk of Maze. Even in the gloom I could see dark patches of sweat forming in a giant V down the back of his shirt as he mopped his brow with one strong forearm.

"Don't you wish my mother and father were here to help you?" I asked, sitting on a pile of old newspapers stacked in one corner. Wind howled over the corrugated roof and made the wooded walls of the shack rattle in their frames. The flame on my candle flickered and I cupped one hand around it to stop it from snuffing out in the draft coming up from beneath the door.

"What?" he asked, looking back over his shoulder at me, and turning the crank on the printer with his giant hands.

"Didn't my mother and father help you produce the newspaper?" I asked him.

"That's right," he said, looking back at the great iron machine before him. The noise from the crank sounded like the bones of a skeleton being jangled together.

"Don't you wish they were here now?" I asked. I knew my uncle didn't want to talk about my parents, but I did. I couldn't let it go – I couldn't let them go. They were my parents and I loved them. I felt somehow lost without them.

"I guess," he grunted, brushing a mop of sweat-soaked hair from his brow.

"When do you think they will come back?" I asked.

"Stop talking and give me a hand over here," he said without looking back at me.

Placing the candle down onto the pile of newspapers I'd been sitting on, I got up and crossed the shack to where my uncle stood stooped over the printer. I could see sheets of off-white coloured paper appear from between two huge black drums that were coated black with sticky-looking ink. The faster Uncle Sidney turned the crank, the quicker the sheets of paper slid from between the rollers.

"Don't just stand their gawping," he remarked. "Collect up the sheets of paper and place them in that box at your feet."

I looked down to see a large wooden crate. Holding out my hands, I gathered up the sheets of paper that streamed from beneath the press and placed them into the box. Each side was covered in rows and rows of typed writing. The light from the nearby candle was too dim for me to read what the tiny rows of printed words said.

And just like I had once wondered what the point had been in my father and mother chasing shadows, I looked at my uncle and said, "What is the point in working so hard to make a newspaper?"

"The people of this town have to get their news somehow, don't they?" he said, glancing at me, then back at the printer.

"News about what?" I wondered.

"About what's happening in England," he said.

"And what is happening?" I asked.

"It's not important – you're too young to understand," he said without glancing up at me.

"I'm nine years old," I said, placing more sheets of the paper into the box. "I'm old enough to understand that you're keeping something from me."

"Like what?" His response was short – snappy.

"Like you know what has happened to my mother and father," I said. Then without any warning, a flood of tears burst onto my cheeks in warm streaks. "I know that they went because of me..."

Slowly my uncle began to stop the crank and the printer grew to a grinding halt. Then scooping me up into his powerful arms, he hugged me tight to him. "Your mother and father didn't leave because of anything you did," he whispered.

"Why then?" I sobbed into his chest.

"They chose to go away," he said.

"Why?"

"Because..." he started, then trailed off.

Easing myself back from his solid chest, I looked into his face. His usually light blue eyes looked clouded over somehow.

"They went away to find out what really happened to the werewolves and vampires," I said.

Slowly, he nodded.

"See? It was my fault they went away," I said, pulling free of his hold.

"How do you figure that?" he asked with a bemused frown.

"I scoffed at them for wasting their lives trying to search for her... to prove she existed..."

"Who?" my uncle broke in.

"The young woman who saved..."

As if suddenly realising who I was talking about, my uncle reached out, placing one thick finger against my lips, preventing me from saying anything more about her. "Shhh," he whispered. Then taking my hand in his he led me from the shack and back through a pile of scattered rubble toward his house.

"What about the newspaper?" I asked him.

"It can wait until tomorrow," he said. "I don't know about you but I feel half-starved and tired. Let's have some supper and then some sleep."

At the door of his ramshackle house that he had taken as his own, I said, "So will you ever tell me where my parents have gone?"

"One day," he said, leading me inside and closing the door behind us.

Chapter Three

Another ten years passed before my uncle told me the truth about my mother and father's disappearance. I believe he only did so because of what I'd discovered. I spent those ten years between my parents' disappearance and discovering the truth living in my uncle's house and helping him to crank out his weekly newspaper. It wasn't a newspaper as such, more like a small pamphlet. But the townsfolk of Maze faithfully brought a copy each week, and this is how my uncle made a small but comfortable living for the both of us. While he sat at his desk and wrote the articles for the paper, I would sit cross-legged before the fire and fold the sheets of printed paper together. When the electricity came on we worked in the glare of a small lamp. When the electricity went out, we worked in the dim glow of candlelight. My uncle continued with my education at home, teaching me how to better read and write. Sometimes my uncle would go away for two or three days at a time and leave me alone. It didn't bother me much. In fact, I enjoyed having the little house to myself. I had become close to a guy named Flint. He was a night-watchman and a year older than me. Some nights when my uncle was away, Flint would come and watch over me for the night. Wrapped in his arms, I didn't feel quite so alone. He was the first and only man I had ever slept with. I couldn't say that I loved him, however much I loved what we did to each other during the secret nights we spent together. I didn't know what my uncle would think of me, if he knew that Flint came to stay while he was away. The only rule my uncle laid down during his absence was that I wasn't allowed into the shack where he kept the printing press. This he kept locked, taking the key with him wherever he went.

I had just turned nineteen, when one morning, as we sat and ate warm toast and drank sweet tea, I asked my uncle where it was he went.

Placing down his chipped cup, he looked across the table at me. "I go in search of stories," he explained. "I seek out other towns, but more than that, I go to the places which were abandoned by humans during the war."

"Why?" I asked.

"So I can report what happened," he said. "It's history – part of our history. We only ever got to this point because what of went before."

"But I've read some of your reports in the newspaper and..." I trailed off.

"And what?" he asked, picking up a thick slice of toast from the cracked plate before him and taking a huge bite. Butter ran over his fingers and down the back of his hand.

"Well, how do you know what you write in your newspaper is true? You can't be sure of any of it. None of us really know what happened to the werewolves and vampires. And besides, what you write isn't exactly news – it's more like history."

"It's news to the people who read my paper," he said. "People are looking for answers – people need that. We need to know our history and how we got to this point. If we understand what happened in the past, it will hopefully help us to be better prepared for the future."

"What do we need to prepare ourselves for?" I asked. I was no longer that naïve nine-year-old girl. I was nineteen – a young woman who was old enough to enjoy the comforts of a lover – and my questions could no longer be so easily pushed aside and left unanswered.

"And that's why I go in search of answers," he said around another mouthful of toast.

"But my mother and father went in search of answers, didn't they?" I asked, pouring myself another cup of tea from the pot. Then glancing up at him and meeting his stare, I added, "And they never came back."

"I come back," he said, taking once last gulp of tea from his cup and standing up.

"But what if one day you don't?" I asked.

He looked hard at me. His face was unreadable.

"Can I come with you next time?" I dared to ask him.

"No," he said with a brisk shake of his head.

"Why not? You know how long I've wanted to write a story for the paper. You know how much I'd like to…"

"There are enough stories in Maze to write about if you really want to contribute to the newspaper," he said, his tone dismissive and unrelenting.

"Like what?" I scoffed back.

"What about the rising crime rate?" he said. "The night-watchmen are small in number and can't cope. Perhaps you could get your *friend* Flint to give you some advice."

How much did he know about Flint? I wondered, my cheeks flushing hot and scarlet. Did my uncle know that Flint and I had become lovers, that we had had sex in his house while he was away? Had he perhaps returned one time without me knowing? Had he heard my cries of joy? I hoped not, but how else did my uncle know about Flint and me? Wouldn't he have said something before? Or perhaps, just as I was feeling now, my uncle had been too embarrassed to say anything. His sudden comment had knocked the wind from me and put me on the back foot. A long, drawn out silence fell between us. As it became almost unbearable, my uncle's face broke out into a warm smile.

"I've got something for you." I watched him reach into the back pocket of his jeans. From it he pulled a tattered-looking paperback. I gasped at the sight of it. I'd never had a book of my own before. Jumping to my feet, I skirted around the table toward him and the book he held in his hands. He gave it to me. The pages were yellow, dog-eared, and turned up. The spine was cracked too, but it didn't matter. I held it carefully, like it was some kind of ancient relic – and in a strange way I knew it was. It had come from a time that had been ravaged and destroyed by beautiful immortals.

I read the title written across the front of the book: *Wuthering Heights* by *Emily Bronte*, it read. "Where did you find it?" I asked without looking up.

"I found it amongst the rubble of some remote farmhouse that I came across the last time I went in search of news," my uncle said.

Carefully, I opened the book. There was an inscription written in black ink on the first page, just below the title. *Happy sixteenth birthday, Andrea – Love from Dad*, it read.

It felt suddenly strange to be holding a book in my hands that had once been given as a birthday present to a girl named Andrea. It had now been given to me as a present, not from my father, but someone I had grown to love just as much.

"Thank you," I breathed, looking up, only to discover that my uncle had gone. I glanced over at the kitchen window to see him heading across the rubble and the yard toward the shack.

Taking the book to my poky bedroom, I lay on the bed and read the book. I read it from cover to cover in one sitting. I couldn't put it down. It was the first book I had ever read. I was gripped not only by the story about Heathcliff and the girl he loved named Catherine, but it gave me a glimpse into the past – into the world that used to be. And for the first time, I truly understood why my mother, father, and uncle wrote the newspaper and why all three of them had gone in search of answers. Answers could be found in books – in the words that had once been written down, just how my uncle now wrote his newspaper. Wasn't he keeping a written record of what the world had once been and what it was now? Did it matter if he got things wrong? The book I'd been holding in my hands had been made up, but it spoke the truth, too. It told the story of love, hate, and betrayal. Of being abandoned as a small child and having to go and live someplace else. In my heart I knew how that felt. The words in the book, although fiction, also spoke a very real truth.

Carefully placing the book to one side, I left the room holding the candle I had lit while reading. I couldn't find my uncle anywhere in the house and I wondered if he wasn't still in the shack working on the next run of his newspaper. It had grown dark, and no sooner had I stepped outside, then my candle was snuffed out by a sudden blast of cold night air. With the candle smouldering in my fist, I stepped over the rubble and crossed the yard to the shack. I knew without opening the door that my uncle wasn't working on the next edition of his newspaper. I couldn't hear the *clank-clank* sound of the printing press spewing out those printed sheets of paper. A crescent shaped moon lit my way as I reached the door. I could hear no sound from the other side of it. Had Uncle Sidney gone off again? I tugged on the latch, and to my surprise the door swung open. I peered into the darkness.

"Uncle?" I whispered over the groaning wind blowing my hair from off my shoulders.

Wondering where my uncle was, I started to swing the door closed, then stopped. The moonlight streaming over my shoulder fell upon the newspapers piled in each corner. These were the overruns and the copies that my uncle had been unable to sell over the years. Stepping into the shack, I plucked up a box of matches from a nearby worktable and lit the candle I had brought with me from the house.

In the orange flare of light, I made my way across to one of the many piles of old newspapers. My uncle had said that he reported the news – it was his mission to keep the townsfolk of Maze up-to-date of what was happening in the world and what had once taken place. Staring at the piles of newspapers, I suddenly couldn't help but wonder if my uncle had ever reported on my parents' disappearance. That had once been news, hadn't it? How could my uncle not have reported the fact that two of the reporters from the newspaper he wrote had suddenly gone missing – vanished?

But where to look? I thought, turning around and looking at the mountains of old newspapers that spanned at least the ten years I had been living with my uncle. Then, spying a pile of faded newspapers in the furthest corner of the shack, I could remember sitting there and watching my uncle work at the printing press. All the other newspapers piled high around me had been produced since that time. So the pile I had sat on as a child would surely be the place to start looking. Setting the candle to one side, I made my way amongst the newspapers. Reaching down, I shifted some of them aside and checked the dates printed in the right-hand corner on each of them. The copies I held in my hand were dated just two years after being taken in by my uncle. I lifted more from the pile, working my way down until I reached the copies that were dated the year my parents had gone missing. Finding them, and with my heart suddenly beating faster than it had ever had, I snatched several editions from the top of the pile. I thumbed through them until I found the copy that my uncle had produced the week my parents had gone missing. Placing the others aside, I read the black printed headline across the top of the front page: **The People of Shade Go Missing!** the headline read.

'Werewolves of Shade'

(The Beautiful Immortals)

Book One

Now Available to download in eBook, paperback and audible edition.

More books by Tim O'Rourke

Kiera Hudson Series One
Vampire Shift (Kiera Hudson Series 1) Book 1
Vampire Wake (Kiera Hudson Series 1) Book 2
Vampire Hunt (Kiera Hudson Series 1) Book 3
Vampire Breed (Kiera Hudson Series 1) Book 4
Wolf House (Kiera Hudson Series 1) Book 5
Vampire Hollows (Kiera Hudson Series 1) Book 6

Kiera Hudson Series Two
Dead Flesh (Kiera Hudson Series 2) Book 1
Dead Night (Kiera Hudson Series 2) Book 2
Dead Angels (Kiera Hudson Series 2) Book 3
Dead Statues (Kiera Hudson Series 2) Book 4
Dead Seth (Kiera Hudson Series 2) Book 5
Dead Wolf (Kiera Hudson Series 2) Book 6
Dead Water (Kiera Hudson Series 2) Book 7
Dead Push (Kiera Hudson Series 2) Book 8
Dead Lost (Kiera Hudson Series 2) Book 9
Dead End (Kiera Hudson Series 2) Book 10

Kiera Hudson Series Three
The Creeping Men (Kiera Hudson Series Three) Book 1
The Lethal Infected (Kiera Hudson Series Three) Book 2
The Adoring Artist (Kiera Hudson Series Three) Book 3
The Secret Identity (Kiera Hudson Series Three) Book 4
The White Wolf (Kiera Hudson Series Three) Book 5

Werewolves of Shade
Werewolves of Shade (Part One)
Werewolves of Shade (Part Two)

Werewolves of Shade (Part Three)
Werewolves of Shade (Part Four)
Werewolves of Shade (Part Five)
Werewolves of Shade (Part Six)

Moon Trilogy
Moonlight (Moon Trilogy) Book 1
Moonbeam (Moon Trilogy) Book 2
Moonshine (Moon Trilogy) Book 3

The Jack Seth Novellas
Hollow Pit (Book One)
Seeking Cara (Book Two) Coming Soon!

Black Hill Farm (Books 1 & 2)
Black Hill Farm (Book 1)
Black Hill Farm: Andy's Diary (Book 2)

Sydney Hart Novels
Witch (A Sydney Hart Novel) Book 1
Yellow (A Sydney Hart Novel) Book 2

The Doorways Saga
Doorways (Doorways Saga Book 1)
The League of Doorways (Doorways Saga Book 2)
The Queen of Doorways (Doorways Saga Book 3)

The Tessa Dark Trilogy
Stilts (Book 1)
Zip (Book 2)

The Mechanic
The Mechanic

The Dark Side of Nightfall
The Dark Side of Nightfall (Book One)
The Dark Side of Nightfall (Book Two)

Unscathed
Written by Tim O'Rourke & C.J. Pinard

Also by Tim O'Rourke writing as Jamie Drew
The November lake Mysteries
November Lake Teenage Detective (Book One)
November Lake Teenage Detective (Book Two)

You can contact Tim O'Rourke at
www.kierahudson.com or by email at kierahudson91@aol.com